Nathan blinked then shook his head. Pregnant.

Had he heard correctly? Had she said *pregnant*? Thank goodness he was already sitting down. Pregnant.

She wasn't ill, though, which was a relief.

He'd known there was something different from her appearance. She looked beautiful as always, but now there was a haunting quality to her beauty, a fragility he hadn't seen before. Her cheekbones were more pronounced. Had she lost weight? He reached out to rub his thumb along her face but managed to pull his hand back before making contact.

He hadn't expected her to say she was pregnant. No, she said she thought she was pregnant. What did she mean, *thought*?

He stood up then started to walk from the lounge door to the window several times, barely noticing the view of Russell Square, as he tried to process the information.

Saira was pregnant. Or she thought she could be pregnant. With his baby? Of course with his baby. If she were pregnant he would be the father.

Dear Reader,

I'm thrilled to be publishing my first book with Harlequin. *Baby Surprise for the Millionaire* is the first book I ever finished writing and I was so excited to finally write "The End" on a project.

But I'll let you in on a little secret: this book has been over ten years in the making. I have many barely started drafts on my computer. It wasn't until I decided to have a heroine who shared my ethnicity that the book finally came together and I was compelled to tell Saira and Nathan's story through to the end.

I love second-chance-at-love stories because we get to share a couple's journey as they try to overcome the obstacles that kept them apart in the past, and that's certainly the case for Saira and Nathan. Their story takes them from London to Malta and to the Alps, both of them convinced that a long-term relationship isn't possible. Saira's unexpected pregnancy provides the catalyst for her and Nathan to come together to decide what they really want for their future.

I hope you enjoy reading Saira and Nathan's story as much as I enjoyed writing it.

Much love,

Ruby Basu

Baby Surprise
for the
Millionaire

—

Ruby Basu

HARLEQUIN®

Romance™

Recycling programs for this product may not exist in your area.

ISBN-13: 978-1-335-40702-3

Baby Surprise for the Millionaire

Copyright © 2022 by Ruby Basu

This edition published by arrangement with Harlequin Books S.A.

For questions and comments about the quality of this book, please contact us at CustomerService@Harlequin.com.

Harlequin Enterprises ULC
22 Adelaide St. West, 41st Floor
Toronto, Ontario M5H 4E3, Canada
www.Harlequin.com

Printed in U.S.A.

Ruby Basu lives in the beautiful Chilterns with her husband, two children and the cutest dog in the world. She worked for many years as a lawyer and policy lead in the civil service. As the second of four children, Ruby connected strongly with *Little Women*'s Jo March and was scribbling down stories from a young age. She loves creating new characters and worlds.

Baby Surprise for the Millionaire
is Ruby Basu's debut title for Harlequin!

Visit the Author Profile page at Harlequin.com.

To Gareth; it must be love.

CHAPTER ONE

'I SEE THE prodigal best friend has returned.'

Saira Dey straightened her shoulders. The rich deep timbre of the voice behind her was unmistakable.

Nathan Haynes.

It was inevitable she would see him again at his sister Miranda's engagement party, but in her imagination she was calm and poised, not being jostled for service at an open bar.

Was there any chance she could pretend she couldn't hear him?

Finally getting her Sauvignon, she took a gulp of liquid courage before turning to face him with a bright smile pasted across her face.

'Nathan, how absolutely delightful to see you again. It's been too, too long. How have you been? How is everything?' she said.

He frowned. 'Are you okay? Why are you speaking like that? I thought you'd come back with a broad Texas accent, not received pronunciation.'

'I'm fine.' She laughed self-consciously and spoke in her normal accent. She tended to slip into a 'posh' British accent when she was unusually nervous, but she hadn't expect him to notice. Not after all this time.

She took a couple of centring breaths. This was Nathan Haynes. She'd known him for years. Nothing to be nervous about.

'You look well,' she said.

A complete understatement. He looked amazing. The years had treated him well. Not a single strand of grey was apparent in his lush wavy brown hair. He wore it much shorter now, clipped straight along his nape, more in keeping with the quintessential businessman he was. She missed the overlong, slightly shaggy hairstyle he'd had when they were younger. His hairstyle wasn't the only thing she missed. Always a handsome man, his face had matured. His jaw had narrowed, and his tanned skin was moulded over chiselled cheekbones, emphasising deep-set intelligent blue eyes. But there was a serious expression there now. Gone was the carefree laughter and welcoming demeanour of his youth.

She lifted her hand to his shoulder to help her balance as she stood on tiptoe to give him an air kiss. Her hand tightened briefly, as she admired the breadth of his shoulders. It evoked a fleeting memory of burying her head against his chest, being held in his arms.

The warmth of his hand on her elbow as he steered her away from the bar towards the side of the roof terrace triggered nerve-endings she'd thought were half-dead.

Careful, Saira, she cautioned herself, *you can't go there again.*

But avoiding all conversation was unrealistic. It would be better to get the initial discomfort out of the way.

'Miranda mentioned you've moved back to England,' Nathan said, once they were able to hear themselves better.

'Yes. A few weeks ago now.'

'I'm sorry to hear about your husband. Miranda told me what happened.'

She nodded in acknowledgement, taking a sip of her drink to avoid replying. It had been two years since her husband's accident, but she never knew how to respond to condolences. One of the benefits of returning to England was that hardly anyone knew her history. They'd never met her husband, which meant she didn't have to deal with the sympathetic looks or, worse, the awkward avoidance of eye contact from people who didn't know what to say to a young widow.

'This is a beautiful venue, Nathan,' she said, deliberately changing the subject, gazing round the roof terrace instead.

The view of the River Thames, still visible in the red hues of the setting sun, was magnificent.

Dim lights were strewn across the glass balustrades, reflecting in the water of the roof pool. Blankets had been placed on chairs and couches for when the evening cooled, although the heat lamps would make them unnecessary. They'd thought of everything to make the event perfect.

'Isn't this your flagship hotel?'

Nathan raised his eyebrows. 'I'm surprised you remember. You didn't show much interest when I was buying it.'

'Of course I was interested, Nathan,' she said in surprise. It was the only thing he'd talked about nine years ago. She always tried to support his dreams, even when they'd been taking him away from her. 'I'm sorry if I made you think otherwise.'

She sensed him staring in her direction but purposely concentrated on the view—as if the London skyline had her completely enthralled. It was strange seeing Nathan again after so many years. Part of her looked forward to it, wanting to know whether the man she'd once been close to had changed, but a larger part of her dreaded it. This inevitable tension—the tension from a shared past—was exactly the reason why.

Saira glanced skyward with a small smile of relief when some other guests came up to them, hoping to take the chance to speak to Nathan.

She had to admit Nathan's accusation she hadn't shown much interest wasn't completely unfair. She'd been an engineering student—business and eco-tourism were different languages to her.

Being at university, and free from parental rules for the first time in her life, she'd been too immature to understand the true nature of what Nathan was dealing with. Leaving the financial sector to move into the hospitality industry had been a huge risk for him. It had meant turning his back on his family wealth and the role he'd been born into, for which he was raised, with the expectation that he would take over. Not many twenty-two-year-olds would have been prepared to take those steps.

It was no surprise Nathan had built the Haynes Group into a huge multi-billion-pound enterprise. The hotels and resorts were only a small part of the conglomerate. According to the financial news, Nathan had an almost uncanny ability to forecast consumer desires to exploit the market.

She watched him for a few minutes. People were constantly coming up to speak to him. It wasn't simply his imposing height and tall, athletic frame, accentuated by the perfect tailoring of his tuxedo, which allowed him to command the room.

He was the consummate host, engaging and engaged. Charismatic and debonair. It was like being in the pull of a strong magnet. Hopefully, eight years and her marriage would serve to dull the attractive force which always simmered between them. A resurgence of their sexual attraction was the last thing she needed right now.

Any kind of relationship wasn't on the agenda. She'd been married and, although she'd been incredibly happy, it was safer to put all thoughts of love and marriage behind her. Losing someone she loved had been devastating. It wasn't something she ever wanted to experience again.

She was an independent single woman in charge of her own destiny.

But she had to admit it was more difficult than she expected, being in the same room as Nathan again. Living an ocean away, in the States, she'd been able to put her feelings away. Now that locked box was at risk of opening.

She pressed her hand against the flutters in her stomach. Not wanting to risk Nathan catching her scrutiny, she tore herself away from his dynamic presence. It would be safer to make her way inside, where it was quieter and where Nathan was unlikely to go while most of the guests remained outside, making the most of the warm early September evening.

She went to search for Miranda, not yet having seen her best friend since she'd arrived. She finally came across her on the way to the bathroom.

They shared a long hug, both unable to speak

at first, emotion overwhelming them. Their friendship had been instantaneous the moment they'd met as five-year-olds on their first day at primary school and had lasted despite their going to different secondary schools, different universities and Saira moving to the US. It had been two years since they'd seen each other in person, the last occasion being when Miranda had flown out to support Saira at Dilip's funeral.

Miranda said, 'I can't believe you're here. This is the best thing that's happened in ages.'

'Ahem!' Her new fiancé Steve coughed in mock affront.

Laughing, Miranda made the introductions. 'We have loads to catch up on. Let's grab some food and eat together. You haven't eaten yet, have you?' Miranda asked.

'No, I haven't been here that long.'

They walked arm in arm to the extensive buffet, sensibly laid out inside, where the wind wouldn't cool the food too quickly.

'Are you really back in London for good?' Miranda asked once they were seated.

'For the next few months at least, but I need to find a job soon.'

'Are you staying at your parents' flat?'

Saira grimaced. 'For now, but I'll be moving out soon. My parents left for India a few weeks ago. It's their six months there.'

'Ah, of course. I've always envied how your

parents get to follow the sun,' Miranda said. 'Why won't you stay on at the flat, then?'

'Ravi's there, and I don't think it's the best idea for us to share space. He's always been so overprotective—even more protective than Ajay. It's almost like they forget I'm twenty-eight now and don't need to be looked after. Not that I ever did. But I'll always be their baby sister.'

Miranda laughed. 'Believe me, I know what you mean,' she said with a wink.

'Anyway, I decided it would be easier if I stay at a bed and breakfast instead. It's only for a few weeks until I can find a short-term rental.'

'Way to go, Saira. You've come back a whole new woman,' Miranda said, patting her on the back affectionately.

'What do you mean?'

'You were always such a dutiful daughter, doing whatever your family told you to. It's nice to see you standing up for what you want.'

'Thanks, Miranda. I appreciate you noticing,' she replied in an amused tone. Same old Miranda, still speaking her mind with brutal honesty. It was wonderful. 'I'm not sure moving into a B&B is quite enough to warrant my being considered a new woman.'

'But you don't need to stay at a B&B. I'm sure we can find a room in one of the Haynes Hotels. Where is Nathan? Have you seen him yet? He'll be happy you're here. I know he'll help,' she said, turning towards the roof terrace.

'Oh, no, please. That's not necessary. I'm happy with the place I've chosen. Anyway, I want to hear more about what's been happening with you and I need all the details about your engagement.' Saira smiled at Steve. 'I'm sure I remember you saying you would never marry unless a prince came and swept you off your feet.'

'I think this is my cue to mingle,' Steve said, standing and giving Miranda a quick kiss. 'I'll try and waylay anyone coming in your direction. That way, you and Saira can have a proper catch-up.'

The joy shining out of her friend's eyes as she watched her fiancé walk away warmed Saira's heart. 'I'm so happy for you,' she said, blinking away unexpected tears.

Miranda beamed at her. 'I'm happy too. My parents' divorce pulled the rug out from under me. I didn't realise how much until I met Steve. I almost lost him because I was convinced love didn't exist.'

Saira reached out a hand. 'It sounds wonderfully romantic. Start at the beginning.'

Nathan loved his sister, but at times like this he could wring her neck. She was living in a fantasy world of blissful happiness and wanted everyone to join her in her bubble. Naturally, he would do what he could to make his sister happy, and it was simple enough for him to arrange a place to stay for Saira. But his preference would have been to keep his interactions with Saira brief and impersonal.

He'd done his duty when he welcomed Saira to the party. The only reason he made his way directly to her the moment he spotted her was that it was always best to get difficult situations over and done with. The abrupt end to their conversation was for the best, and he didn't have any inclination to speak to her again. If the tension in his jaw was any indication, he was still annoyed about the way things had ended, even if it had been eight years ago.

Life was good. His family were content. He had female companionship when he wanted it without any strings to tie him down. His business was more successful than ever and, if he were able to complete this latest project before Christmas, the Haynes Group would be the biggest developer of luxury eco-resorts in the world.

Saira was the only small blot on his horizon.

He'd contacted his executive assistant to book out a suite for her at his Haynes Mayfair, London hotel. Now he needed to seek her out to let her know. He supposed he could pass the information on via Miranda, but it would probably be easier if he did it directly.

He sensed the moment she came back out onto the terrace, his gaze automatically going to her. She was beautiful, framed by the lights strewn across the trellis. Tiny tendrils escaped from the mass of raven hair she'd swept into a knot, framing her oval face. Even from a distance he could see the skilfully applied make-up shadowing her features, emphasising her cheekbones. Had she had her make-up done professionally? The girl he had known never wore any, her fresh-faced complexion not needing it. But that was years ago.

The cocktail dress she wore draped over her curves, showing off her trim waist. For a petite person she had surprisingly long legs, their slim length displayed by the above-the-knee hemline of her dress. Red had always been her colour, the perfect complement to her golden-brown complexion.

She stood alone near the doorway, biting her lip and glancing around, not trying to make eye contact. 'Shy' wasn't a word he would use to describe her. She'd never had any problem voicing her opinions to him. But when they were younger she'd taken her time and let the conversation happen around her, observing people before she participated, and she probably didn't know many people at the party, which could explain her uncertainty.

He grabbed two flutes of champagne from

a passing waiter and made his way over. Holding out a flute, he said, 'I've organised a room for you at our Mayfair hotel. You can move in whenever you're ready.'

'What do you mean?' she asked, gazing at him with curiosity in her large brown eyes.

'Miranda asked me to arrange a room at a Haynes Hotel. It's been booked for you,' he replied, checking his watch, then glancing around the room.

Saira sighed. 'Your sister doesn't know how to give up. I honestly didn't ask her to interfere. Thank you for going to all this trouble, but I already have a place to stay.'

'She said you aren't staying at your parents' flat.'

Saira nodded and explained her living situation.

'Are your parents still going out to Kolkata in time for Durga Puja, then?' he asked.

Her mouth broke into a wide, friendly smile. 'You remember?'

'I found it interesting you celebrate Durga Puja, not Diwali. I must have retained the fact.'

Her smile faded as she lowered her head. Was she disappointed by his factual response? She must know what they'd had was in the past, long buried.

'About the room,' he said, trying to end their

conversation. 'It's all organised now. You may as well take it.'

'I don't need it.' Saira sighed again. 'I am grateful to you and Miranda, but it isn't necessary.'

His temple started to throb with irritation. He briefly squeezed his eyes shut and pinched his nose, then, giving her the tight but courteous smile he used during difficult business negotiations he said, 'Miranda asked me to do her a favour and I did. Maybe you should try convincing her you don't need it.'

Saira threw him an amused glance. 'Have you met your sister? You can't convince her of anything.'

His lips twitched involuntarily. 'Exactly, so you may as well give in gracefully and accept the room.'

'The path of least resistance?' She nodded. 'I see your point.'

'It would make her happy,' he added.

If Saira was at all like the person she used to be, she wouldn't want to disappoint her friend. He could tell she was weighing up her options. What would she decide, and why did he even care?

'In that case, I accept your offer of a place to stay. Thank you,' she said finally.

His smile was warmer as he handed her a

business card. 'Call this number. My assistant will give you all the details.'

They stood next to each other for a few moments, not saying anything, avoiding each other's eyes. He glanced down—she was resolutely staring ahead. He followed the direction of her gaze to where his sister was laughing with a group of people, her fiancé next to her with his arm around her.

'They look so happy, don't they?' Saira said a little wistfully.

'Yes. Steve's a great guy. Still, I am surprised Miranda thinks she wants to get married.'

Saira expelled an exasperated-sounding breath. 'Well, of course you would be. I still remember your views on marriage. It doesn't sound like they've changed over the years.'

'No, they haven't,' he replied, his voice cold and exact. 'And Miranda used to share my views.'

'Perhaps Miranda's views have matured a bit since she was twenty,' Saira said.

She glared up at him, a glimmer of annoyance sparking fire in her deep, dark eyes. A brief smile touched his lips—it hadn't taken long for her to drop her polite veneer and let her acerbic tongue reappear.

'If you ask me, it's hope triumphing over experience,' he replied.

'Experience?' She gave a loud, disbelieving laugh. 'You mean your parents?'

'Not only them. I'm sure I don't have to tell

you about the statistics for unsuccessful marriages.'

She narrowed her eyes. 'I'm guessing you
haven't shared your opinions with Miranda? I
mean, she still seems to be talking to you.'

'Of course I haven't.'

He couldn't and wouldn't say anything to
convince Miranda not to get married. After
the break-up of their parents' marriage they'd
become disillusioned with the idea of happily-
ever-after. Something had changed, and Miranda seemed happy now, but it had taken her
a long time to find personal happiness. They
didn't have any role models for a good lasting
marriage, but perhaps Miranda and Steve would
work at their relationship. All he could do was
support her decisions and be there for her when
it fell apart. The way he had been there for his
mother each time his father had left.

He formed an image of his mother the first
time his father had walked out. Nathan had been
twelve. He'd returned home from school to find
her lying in bed, unable even to get changed.
He never considered his mother to be weak or
dependent—her depressive state had come as a
shock. He tried to protect Miranda from seeing
their mother that way, making meals and helping with her homework until his mother slowly
started trying to get back to normality—only

for his father to waltz back into their lives as if nothing had happened.

That had started a pattern which would last for another ten years. His father would come home, only to leave when he inevitably got bored again. Each time Nathan not only had to pick up his mother but Miranda, and two younger sisters had also been relying on him, crying on his shoulder. He'd even decided to study at Oxford so he could be within a reasonable distance of his family.

The final time his father had left, emigrating to Australia with his latest girlfriend, Nathan had been in his twenties. It had been almost a relief when his mother had received the divorce papers—at least he wouldn't be back in their lives.

After seeing first-hand the damage his father's actions had inflicted on his mother, on his family, Nathan would never put himself—or anyone else—in that situation. He ensured his relationships were short-term, moving on before there was any emotional involvement. There was no promise of love. No fiction of happily-ever-after.

'Well, I'm pleased you're managing to hide your pessimism so well,' Saira said, interrupting his thoughts.

'I would never do anything to upset Miranda. I would do anything for my sisters.'

'I know. And you always go above and beyond.

You gave her this engagement party,' she said, gesturing round the room. 'It really is amazing.'

And suddenly he watched the fight go out of her. She was once again a polite stranger, turning back to stare around the room, anywhere but at him.

He pressed his lips together. This chilly atmosphere between them wasn't ideal. Miranda hadn't set a wedding date yet, but Nathan had offered to pay for everything, which meant he would probably have some involvement with the arrangements. Now Saira was back in London, Miranda would want her best friend to be part of the wedding preparations. Avoiding her wasn't a realistic or practical option, even though it would be his preference.

He closed his eyes briefly in resignation. He would do anything to ensure nothing spoiled his sister's happiness.

'Saira, with Miranda's wedding coming up, I'm sure we're going to see each other occasionally. Perhaps we should have coffee some time to talk…try to find a way to get past our issues.'

She looked up at him in surprise. 'You think we have issues left to resolve?'

'No, I think this awkwardness is perfectly normal for two people who pretty much grew up with each other.'

Saira raised her eyebrows at the clear sarcasm. Nathan had been polite and distant during most of their conversation. She'd assumed he felt nothing for her, but it sounded as if he was angry. That was crazy. If anyone had the right to be angry it was her. Clearly he was right—they did have issues to resolve.

They were interrupted by Miranda, who flung her arms round them both. 'Two of my favourite people right here. Together. Nathan, can you believe we have our Saira back?'

'Yes, it's great,' he replied. The lack of enthusiasm in his voice belied his words. 'Are you a bit tipsy?'

'No!' Miranda laughed. 'I'm so, so incredibly happy. I'm going to marry the best man in the world. I have the best brother, and my best friend is back in London. Could anything make this more perfect? I wish we had more chance to talk.'

'That's the problem with being the popular one,' Saira said, putting her arm round Miranda's waist. 'But don't worry. I'm going to be around for a while. We can catch up soon.'

'Not soon enough. Day after tomorrow, we're going to be away for ages,' Miranda said with a pout.

'Okay then, let's arrange a date for as soon as you get back.'

'No, I don't want to wait,' Miranda replied.

'There's nothing you can do about it,' Nathan said.

Miranda gave a moue of disappointment, then

a bright smile crossed her face. 'Yes, I can,' she said. 'Saira can come with us.'

'I am not going on a romantic holiday with you and Steve,' Saira said, her voice rising in horror.

'It's not a romantic holiday. At least not for the first few days. We're going to one of Nathan's new resorts, with him and his uni buddies. It's a diving holiday. You should come along.'

Nathan's grimace was a clear indication he wasn't happy with his sister's suggestion. 'I still can't gate-crash,' Saira said. 'It's obviously been arranged for a long time. Besides, I don't know how to dive.'

'Neither do I,' Miranda replied. 'This is even more perfect. Now I don't have to be bored while the others do their dives. They go on holiday every year in September. It's not a special one-off event. And I need someone I can chat to properly. Some of the other girlfriends who go… well, the nicest way to say it is we don't have much in common. You'll be doing me a favour. We can catch up over cocktails at the beach and spend time in the spa getting mani-pedis or massages.'

'That sounds lovely, but it must be too late to get flights and rooms.' Saira silently appealed to Nathan for support.

'The hotel is booked up and all the huts we're staying at are already taken,' Nathan confirmed.

'Then Saira can stay on the pull-out bed in my hut.'

'I am not staying with you and Steve!' Saira protested, laughing at Miranda's insistence. Her friend didn't know when to quit.

Miranda was quiet for a moment. 'Then she can stay with you,' she said to Nathan. 'You're between girlfriends, aren't you? You're not bringing anyone on this trip.'

Saira and Nathan exchanged glances.

'Please, Nathan,' Miranda implored.

'I suppose Saira could stay in my hut,' he said after a long pause, surprising Saira with his easy capitulation to his sister's request. 'I'll speak to one of the others, see whether I can bunk with them. We're only there for four nights anyway.'

'Then it's all settled,' Miranda said with satisfaction. 'I'm going to tell Steve the wonderful news.'

Saira watched as Miranda walked away. She turned to Nathan. 'Wow, your sister's still a bulldozer, I see.'

'Miranda likes being in control.'

'Really?' Saira smiled. 'Thanks for the information, pot.'

'What's that supposed to mean?'

'Being in control is a Haynes family trait.'

'I don't think that's a completely fair assessment.'

Saira sighed. She'd offended him. Would they

ever be able to have a normal conversation? It was a good job she wasn't really going on holiday with them, even if it were practically possible.

'What are the chances of Miranda forgetting about this holiday?'

'None. You may as well start packing.'

Saira laughed. 'You're going away the day after tomorrow—surely there's no way I could get a plane ticket.'

'That's not a problem. I presume you have a valid passport?'

'Of course.'

'Then reconcile yourself to coming on this holiday. When you contact my assistant, he can give you the full details of the flights and anything you need to know.'

Saira shook her head. 'I don't know if it's a good idea. Particularly if you're single. Miranda is so loved up she probably thinks we should be together.'

'Perhaps. But that's because she doesn't know.'

'Know what?'

'We've already tried that and failed. Twice.'

CHAPTER TWO

A HUT!

Saira couldn't believe Nathan had referred to this accommodation as a hut. The only similarity between her definition of a hut and the bungalow suites at the Haynes Malta Beach Resort was their construction material.

It was the kind of place that didn't need 'luxury' in its title. Even without the Haynes branding, the resort was a piece of paradise sprawled across a private island close to Gozo. Their accommodation, the Beach Huts, was a group of six bungalows set apart from the main hotel with their own private facilities.

It felt surreal that she was there. Life really did fall into place when you had almost unlimited wealth. Plane tickets weren't a problem when you owned a private jet.

Inside the bungalow there was a large bedroom with an en suite bathroom. The living area was spacious, with a comfortable-looking sofa and armchair, a small dining table and a fully stocked bar and kitchen area with a fridge, microwave and tea-making facilities. She walked towards the trifold windows at the back of the living space, which led to a deck with seating, a hot tub and plunge pool.

She exhaled, her shoulders loosening as she envisaged spending her time by the pool, sipping a glass of wine while gazing at the sparkling turquoise waters of the Mediterranean.

'I presume you expect me to be a gentleman and offer you the bed, don't you?'

Nathan's voice interrupted her inspection. Her shoulders tightened again immediately. The only slight cloud over this holiday was having to share the bungalow with Nathan. Unfortunately, since his friends had all brought their current partners, and neither she nor Nathan wanted to impose on the couples, they'd agreed to share his suite.

She'd tried to back out of the holiday, tried to persuade Miranda it was a bad idea. She'd caved under Miranda's insistence on wanting to spend time reconnecting with her friend—according to Miranda she would only be happy on holiday if Saira were there too.

If Saira was honest with herself, she was curious to discover how much Nathan had changed from the young man she'd known. It was for less than five days, after all. At least the sofa in the lounge pulled out into a bed, so there was no risk they'd have to share.

'No, I expect nothing from you, Nathan,' she replied, rolling her eyes before turning from the windows to give him a sweet, clearly false smile. 'I'm happy to take the pull-out. You're offering me a holiday, after all.'

'That was Miranda's idea.'

'I know, but you agreed. You didn't have to.'

Nathan probably didn't realise how kind he'd been—arranging somewhere for her to stay in London, letting her come on the holiday in the first place, even sharing his bungalow with her. Miranda had asked him so, as always, he'd gone out of his way to make his sister happy.

'I'm sure I could have stayed at the hotel,' Saira said.

'The hotel is a ten-minute drive from here and the facilities are completely separate, although we can use them. It's more convenient for everyone if you to stay here.'

She sank into the couch, then stretched her legs in front of her. Nathan was still standing near the entrance to the guesthouse, stiff and uncomfortable. She closed her eyes. She should have insisted she stay somewhere else. But it would have been difficult to refuse to share with Nathan without giving a good excuse to Miranda, who didn't know about their past relationship.

Saira bit her lip. 'I'm sorry, Nate. You won't be able to relax if we're sharing. I don't want to spoil your holiday with your friends. Perhaps I should stay at the hotel.'

There was an almost imperceptible sigh before he walked over to sit in an adjoining armchair.

'The hotel is at capacity. I guess we can make the best of a difficult situation,' he said in clipped tones.

'Ah, I forgot how much of a charmer you are.' She smiled brightly as he briefly pursed his lips, barely able to conceal his irritation.

'Well, pardon me for finding it awkward sharing a room with my ex-girlfriend.'

'Ex-girlfriend? Is that how you think of me?'

'I've barely thought of you since you ran away to America.'

Saira frowned. Ran away? That was a surprising choice of words. Did he honestly see what had happened as running away? She'd always been going to study in the States as part of her degree. Perhaps she had travelled abroad a little earlier than planned, when he told her there was no long-term future for them, but it had been the best thing for her to do.

'That was lifetimes ago,' she said simply, rather than indulging her curiosity by asking him to explain himself.

But he'd brought up their awkward situation again. And it was true. It *was* awkward, because nobody, including Miranda, knew about their previous relationship—or Saira was sure Miranda would never have suggested they share. There was history between them. They couldn't get away from it.

'Look, you mentioned we should chat, clear the air. Perhaps we should do that now.'

'Now?' he asked.

'It seems as good a time as any.'

'If you want.'

She closed her eyes and counted to ten, then counted to ten again. The entire time she'd known him it had never been about what *she* wanted. She expelled a deep breath.

'Saira,' Nathan said, breaking into her thoughts, 'this doesn't need huge introspection. We don't have to rehash every detail of our past. I meant we should acknowledge it, draw a line under it and move on.'

'"Past is prologue,"' she murmured.

'I don't think Shakespeare's relevant here. My priority is Miranda. She's been through a lot and I don't want anything to spoil her wedding plans. Let's be realistic. Miranda will want you involved with her wedding, probably in the wedding party. That means we need to get along somehow.'

'I agree. Miranda is our priority. But we can't pretend the past didn't happen. We were young, but we were together for a while, and neither of us can pretend it ended well. You even said at the party we had issues we need to resolve.'

'I didn't mean doing a forensic analysis going into excruciating detail. It's not necessary.'

She threw her hands up in exaggerated despair. 'Why am I surprised? It has to be your way, doesn't it?'

Nathan frowned. 'It's not about that. Tell me what purpose dredging through the past will serve.' He barely glanced in her direction.

'Well, how else do we resolve our issues?'

'Draw a line under them.'

'How do you suggest we do that if we don't talk about them?' She could hear herself almost whining in frustration.

'It's quite simple. We agree that the past is in the past. It has no bearing on what we need to do for Miranda's sake. Anything more is unnecessary. There's no need to blow this out of proportion.'

She was about to insist that discussing their past was a proportional response, then changed her mind. He wasn't going to listen. What was the point?

He continued, 'It was over between us a long time ago. You've been married since then.'

'And you've had a revolving door of relationships,' she bit out.

They locked eyes, neither willing to be the first to break the contact, not quite at war but in a battle for dominance. That was the only reason her breath was coming a little faster. Nothing to do with the sensation of drowning in deep blue eyes with hues rivalling the Mediterranean.

They were interrupted by Nathan's mobile. Glancing at the number, he apologised before turning his back on her to take the call.

'Sorry,' he said again a few moments later. 'There's something urgent I have to deal with. Can we talk about this later?'

'Sure.' It wasn't as if she had a choice.

He ran his hands through his hair, the only visible indication their exchange had affected him at all. 'I'm going to be working until lunch. My friends and I prefer to eat meals together when we're on holiday, because we've carved out this time especially to spend it together. After that I may need to do some more work, but I will make some time to talk later.'

Saira shrugged. She admired his dedication to maintaining his friendships but was still slightly disappointed he wouldn't stop working. He used to complain about his father never spending time with his family on holiday.

Besides, if Nathan refused to discuss the past fully what was there left to talk about? But this wasn't the right time to go into it.

'Fine,' she said. 'Until we've had a chance to talk let's try to be on friendlier terms, particularly in front of Miranda. We don't want her to worry about us. Deal?' She extended her hand.

He glanced at her hand. His upper lip twitched, then he reached out to shake. 'Deal.'

Her hand was enveloped by his larger one, strong and firm. His nails were neatly manicured. She had always loved his hands. His fingers were long and shapely, almost artistic. She remembered his fingers running over the piano keyboard as he played a piece he'd composed. Those same fingers strumming her body, easily finding all the right notes.

Nathan tugged his hand. She released it immediately. How mortifying to hold on longer than necessary.

She stood and walked over to the windows, opened the trifold doors and stepped onto the deck. The warmth of the Maltese afternoon hit her strongly after the air-conditioned room, matching the heat in her cheeks.

She needed to avoid spending much time alone with Nathan. She was already staring at him far too often and he'd notice if she wasn't careful. He probably wouldn't understand that she was only searching for remnants of the young man she'd once known. This cool, detached man he presented to her, and to the world, was mostly a stranger.

She held a hand to her heart reflexively, experiencing a momentary pang for a lost love. It would be too easy to confuse the present with her memories of being nineteen again, experiencing the thrill of falling intellectually and passionately in love for the first time.

This wouldn't do. If she was beginning to relive emotions from a love affair that had ended eight years ago, it would be safer for her if Nathan remained a stranger.

Nostalgia wasn't welcome—for either of them. Too much water and all that.

He was right. There was no point raking over the frozen coals of their past. They never had a shared future.

She'd already decided to be independent. To focus on her career. Romance wasn't part of that. She'd returned to England so she could move on with her life. That life didn't include Nathan— not then and not now.

She stepped back inside as their cases were delivered. Nathan was working on his laptop when she took her case through to the bedroom to change. The flight had only taken three hours and, because they had flown in a private plane, they were able to land directly on the island's airstrip rather than flying into Malta then taking the ferry to Gozo and another boat to the island.

She still wanted to get out of the clothes she'd travelled in, which were better suited to the late-summer weather in England than the glorious temperature of the Mediterranean.

Checking her watch, she picked out a bikini and a simple sundress. There was still an hour before she'd agreed to meet Miranda for lunch. She would take her e-reader and sit by the pool, perhaps have a swim.

Nathan was still working, barking orders at someone down the phone, and didn't notice when she left.

She chose a lounger and started to arrange her things before being interrupted almost immediately by an attendant, who set up her sun lounger, laid out towels, adjusted the parasol and showed her a fridge with water and soft drinks. He handed her a cocktail and snacks menu before leaving her with a pager.

She wasn't sure if the high level of attention was because she was the only one out there. She had to admit she was looking forward to getting to know Nathan's friends—the people Nathan chose to have in his life. She had seen them on the plane but hadn't had the chance to talk to them.

Nathan and his friends were all exceptionally handsome men in their early thirties. The five of them were also wealthy and unmarried, so naturally they'd caught the attention of the press. A tabloid had noticed the five bachelors met regularly—once in September, for a holiday, and again in March for the Talbot family's Spring Ball. Their meet-ups gained interest because they were always with a new partner at each semi-annual event. Because of this, the media had dubbed them 'The Six-Month Men'.

Saira couldn't imagine starting a relationship with someone when you knew it was likely to end within six months. Either the partners foolishly thought they could change their man, or they were also only after something short term.

She'd never had a fling. She'd gone from her relationship with Nathan to her marriage. Perhaps she should add a fling to her list, now she was in control of her own decisions, no longer needing to account to anyone else.

She scrunched her nose. There was a lot to do to get her life on track—having a fling could stay off the list.

Nathan glanced at his watch. Four o'clock. Work had taken longer to deal with than he expected. Usually he enjoyed the intellectual challenge, finding solutions to intractable problems. But today it had been more frustrating than invigorating.

His satisfied gaze went around the fully serviced business suite he'd been using since after lunch. Nathan wanted his resorts to be primarily family-friendly places, to relax and unwind, but he ensured each one had a business centre for people to keep on top of work if they needed.

Nathan might not believe in love or want a family—he'd been told often enough he was too much like his father to take that risk—but his vision was to have resorts where all facilities were available. That way work would never be an excuse to stop anyone coming on holiday and spending time with the people they cared about. Unlike his own father, who had always managed to be dealing with a work crisis whenever they were due to go away. By the time Nathan's younger sisters had been born there hadn't even been any pretence his father would join them on their family holidays.

He grimaced. This annual holiday with his friends was a testament to the fact that people could make time if it was important enough. They all knew the pressures and burdens of running large organisations, but none of them wanted to be the kind of person who let his friendships fade because of work or success. So far none of them had failed to turn up for their annual September holiday.

He left the business centre and took a buggy back to the bungalows. The unexpected sight of Saira on a lounger by the poolside, surrounded by his friends, stopped him in his tracks.

He should have expected this. He didn't regret giving in to Miranda's request for Saira to join them, even if it meant sharing his accommodation. His sister's happiness at having her best friend around was evident—any uncomfortable moments he might feel were worth it for that alone. But he hadn't fully considered the interest Saira's presence would create. Of course his friends would remember her name from eight years ago, even though they'd never met her before today.

He stood at the side for a few minutes, observing the group. He barely noticed his friends' partners around the pool, his gaze invariably going to Saira. The shadows moving across her face threw her cheekbones into stark relief, emphasising her delicate beauty.

She laughed. His breath caught.

He remembered that laugh—would recognise it anywhere…could pick it out in a crowd. It was deep, throaty, full-hearted. Over lunch he'd heard her quieter laugh, the one she used when she was amused but didn't want to bring attention to herself. But, although he listened out, he hadn't heard her other kinds of laughter. Like her infectious giggles when something punny tickled her, or her gravelly laugh, bordering on evil, when something was a bit naughty or risqué.

Was it possible to miss someone's laugh? He would go out of his way to hear all her different laughs. Which was ridiculous. Whatever they'd meant to each other was in the past and she meant nothing to him now. He always needed to remember that.

It didn't surprise him that she'd managed to captivate his friends. These men were like brothers to him. They supported each other and were always there for each other. He would trust them with his life.

But that didn't mean he wanted them interrogating Saira.

He walked over to the group. Almost immediately the others moved away, giving them privacy. Nathan frowned. He didn't want anyone reading into his relationship with her. Surely lunch had proved there was nothing between them—that she was nothing more than his sister's best friend, practically a stranger.

The only seat available for him at the table had been opposite her, but they'd barely interacted. She'd spent most of her time speaking with Miranda, answering questions from the others, not even glancing in his direction, and never making eye contact. Unfortunately, judging by his knowing smile his friend, Bastien Talbot, who had sat next to her, had caught Nathan staring at her.

'Is everything all right?' Nathan asked now, sitting on the side of the lounger next to her so he could face her directly.

'Yes, it's been perfect. Really relaxing,' she replied.

He stared, transfixed, as she stretched. Her sundress was moulded to her body, damp from when she'd gone for a swim.

'How about you? Did you get your work done?' He glanced away quickly. Had she noticed his appraisal? 'Yes, for now,' he replied. 'I'm hoping to finalise a few deals today, which means I won't be disturbed while we're diving. I'll probably have to work before and after dinner, though. Where are Miranda and Steve?' he asked, not seeing them round the pool.

'They went for a walk round the resort. I think they wanted to be alone.'

She gave him the barest hint of a wink, but the humour in her expression brought back memories of the way she'd looked when they were younger.

He smiled at her, not anticipating his visceral, yet familiar reaction when she beamed a smile in return. She was still a beautiful woman—he was having the normal reaction of a healthy straight male. That didn't mean there were any residual feelings between them.

For his sister's sake, and their own, they needed to find a way to put the past behind them—to make sure there wasn't any awkwardness between them when they were around other people. Only then would they be able to treat each other as casual acquaintances, the same way he treated all of his sisters' other friends. Forget they had ever been more to each other.

But that conversation wasn't going to be an enjoyable experience when Saira gave him the impression she wanted to dredge up and analyse their past in detail. As if she had no understanding of what her leaving him had done.

No. Rehashing their former relationship wouldn't help either of them. Some things were better left unsaid.

His lips twitched as he recalled her quoting Shakespeare. His mother loved her for sharing the same passion for the Bard as she did. Luckily Saira had promised never to copy his mother in naming her daughters after characters from the plays…

He mentally gave himself a shake. The names of her future children were of no concern to him.

'Are you all right?'

Her voice interrupted his thoughts. Her quizzical expression made it clear he'd been quiet for a while.

'Yes, I'm fine. We still need to find time to have that talk.'

'I've been thinking about this, and you're right.'

He raised his eyebrows at that unexpected response. 'You never think I'm right.'

'That's because you rarely are,' she replied with a smirk.

'What am I right about this time?'

'Our talk. I'm overcomplicating things.' She frowned. 'It's not like either of us has any lurking resentment about the past. We've both moved on so, unless there's something you want to bring up about our relationship, we can simply draw a line under it like you suggest.'

He stayed silent. He wasn't convinced she was accurate in her assertion that he didn't have any 'lurking resentment', but she was right—they had both moved on.

'Agreed.' He grimaced at the terseness in his tone. 'We're both adults and can be civil in each other's company.'

'Civil?' She sounded amused. 'We used to get on well. I was hoping we could at least try to be friends by the end of the holiday.'

Friends? He briefly considered whether a friendship with Saira was possible. Instinctively he knew it would be difficult. He was still experiencing some kind of attraction, but whether it was to the person she was now or a residue from their past he wasn't sure. And there wasn't any point delving into it. She was a marriage kind of person and he steered clear of long-term commitment. There had never been any future for them and friendship might cause lines to blur.

'Are you hungry?' he asked. 'I can arrange a light afternoon tea… I'll be honest, Saira. I don't know if we can ever be friends, but I don't want us to be enemies. A walk on the beach and something to eat while we have a quick chat will be a good way to start.'

Saira's furrowed her brow. She opened her

mouth, closed it, then sighed. 'Sure. Give me a moment to change. I'm still damp.'

Her words drew his attention back to the lush curves of her figure in the sundress. His mouth went dry.

'Nathan?' Saira said in a confused tone.

He cleared his throat, prevented from saying anything when Bastien came over to let them know about a beach volleyball game being arranged.

'Saira and I are going for a walk,' Nathan said. 'I'll organise for some afternoon tea to be served on the beach for all of us and we'll meet you for that.'

'I'll join you in a bit,' Saira said, still giving him confused glances.

He watched after her as she walked away.

'So that's the elusive Saira,' Bastien said.

'Hardly elusive,' Nathan scoffed.

'You talked about her all the time but never introduced us.'

'We weren't together until after I left uni, so there was no opportunity to introduce you.' He glanced at his friend. 'And I didn't talk about her *all* the time.'

'Sure you didn't,' Bastien replied with humour in his tone.

'It doesn't matter—it's all in the past.' Where it had to stay.

'Really? Because the rest of us assumed she was out of bounds. But if she's not…'

Despite being fully aware his friend was goading him, he turned to stare at him. 'Don't you have a girlfriend?' he asked, raising an eyebrow.

'For now,' Bastien agreed. 'But who knows what the future holds?'

Nathan narrowed his eyes. 'Well, whatever the future holds, consider her out of bounds. For all of you.'

He walked off, sensing Bastien was grinning after him. He shook his head. It wasn't jealousy that caused his reaction. Saira was his sister's age. He was being protective over her. That was it. He had no other feelings for Saira. He never could.

CHAPTER THREE

WALKING ALONG THE beach with the sun starting to set and the waves crashing over her bare feet should have been incredibly romantic. Instead Saira was tense and uncomfortable. She glanced at the others playing volleyball in the distance, wishing she were with them instead.

She'd agreed to Nathan's suggestion expecting that drawing a line under their past relationship would put an end to the awkwardness. He was right. What good would bringing up the past do? She certainly had no desire to relive that embarrassment and heartbreak.

Apart from occasionally seeing each other for Miranda's wedding arrangements, they wouldn't need to be in each other's company. From his brief mention of her running away, she imagined their memory of what happened was at odds. Rehashing it would only make those occasions they did have to meet more uncomfortable.

Miranda had looked surprised and curious when they told her they were going for a walk on the beach. With hindsight, it did sound like a couple's thing to do. She didn't want anyone to get the wrong impression or speculate there was more to her relationship with Nathan.

While she had been lying by the pool earlier, Bastien had teased her about noticing some sexual tension between her and Nathan over lunch, commenting on their charged looks. Which made no sense. During the meal, whenever she'd looked in Nathan's direction—which had been more often than she cared to admit—he'd been talking to his friends or their partners. He hadn't looked in her direction. Not once. There had been no accidental meeting of the eyes, no longing looks.

There wasn't any sexual tension between Nathan and her. Tension, perhaps, but sexual? No way. Just because she found him incredibly attractive, and her eyes zoomed in on him even among a group of handsome men like his friends, it wasn't enough to create sexual desire.

She turned to look at Nathan, striding beside her in board trunks and a tight T-shirt which accentuated his chiselled biceps. Her heart accelerated. Her skin felt as if it was too tight for her body. She expelled a breath.

She was having a basic physical reaction to the presence of a gorgeous man. She should be relieved she could still experience that kind of reaction. She thought it had died when her husband did.

Attractive didn't equate to *attracted to* in her book. And Nathan definitely didn't have the kind of personality she was attracted to any more.

Nathan was the kind of person who couldn't help taking control. At lunch she'd watched as Nathan took charge of ordering the meals and organising the stay. Even among a group of alpha males he was dominant, the others happily deferring to him, although perhaps that was because they were staying at his resort.

She didn't want that.

Nathan was her past—from when she'd been young and shallow and cared about looks. As she matured, her preference had been for someone she had things in common with. Someone easygoing. Someone who considered her an equal—making plans with her, sharing decision-making. Someone like Dilip.

She stopped to gaze out over the ocean. It had been two years since Dil had passed away. She missed him. But the pain was a little less sharp with each passing day. She needed to move on with her life. She was ready to move on.

Her first step had been returning to England. Now she wanted to be independent. She *needed* to be independent.

There was no time—no inclination—for a relationship. How could she allow anyone else in?

Losing love was devasting and she'd experienced it twice. She didn't have the strength to risk her heart again.

She had no interest in any kind of relationship at all—not with alpha, beta or even omega males.

All she had to do was keep her body under control.

Despite their intention to deal quickly with their former relationship, they hadn't spoken much since they'd started walking. One of them needed to make the first move.

'You said a quick chat would be a good idea?' she began, not intending it to sound like a question.

'Yes. It sounds as though we're both on the same page, which makes it easier. Our priority is Miranda.'

She nodded.

'Few people know we were together. Nobody else needs to know. It was a long time ago and we were both much younger. It wasn't a big deal. I see no need to rehash what happened and the whys and the wherefores.'

Not a big deal? Wasn't that part of the problem—their past relationship might have been insignificant to him, but it had been a big deal to her.

'I see,' she replied. 'I've already said I agree with you. I don't see the point of this talk.'

Nathan took a deep breath. 'You may have

said it, but you're still tense in my company and that's going to make the others uncomfortable.'

'I'm not,' she lied. 'Why would I be? As you say, it was years ago. I'm over it. I've been married since then. I think that makes it obvious it's in the past. And I was just one in a long line of women for you. Why would that make me tense?'

Nathan came to an abrupt halt and turned her towards him. Sensations ran through her body from the points on her upper arm where his fingers touched her.

'That kind of remark is what I mean. You make digs about my relationships. It suggests you're bothered.'

She laughed. 'I couldn't care less. Come on— it's not as if I'm the only person who comments on the longevity of your girlfriends. You and your friends are well known as the Six-Month Men.'

It had been easier to talk when they were side by side. Face to face it was harder to hide her feelings. She made sure to maintain a blank expression.

'I promise you, Nathan, we're on the same page. I may not be happy with the way we ended things, but I'm absolutely fine we did end.'

He narrowed his eyes. 'Are you sure?'

She laughed. 'Of course I'm sure. If you don't like me teasing you about the six-month thing then I won't. Past may be prologue, but it's still the past. Whatever happened between us then, now you're just my best friend's brother. Nothing more.'

He searched her face. She met his gaze unflinchingly. He gave a brief nod and they turned forward to continue their walk.

'Good,' he said. 'That's all settled, then.'

She breathed out. Her arms still felt the imprint of his hands. Was that normal when you felt nothing for a person?

Worried about the direction her thoughts were taking, she searched for a neutral topic. 'This is a beautiful place,' she said, before segueing into questions about his other resorts.

'What you're doing is amazing,' she said, after he'd described his new projects.

Although he'd spoken in brief, concise statements, she had sensed his underlying passion. She'd always admired his strong work ethic, his determination to succeed on his own terms, but she hadn't realised what a visionary he was, with his emphasis on ensuring his hotels were ecologically sustainable and researching carbon-neutral travel.

'Your family must be exceedingly proud of you,' she said without thinking.

He frowned, as if the thought never occurred to him. 'Only Miranda has visited any of the Haynes Hotels outside England. Mum won't travel, and Beatrice and Juliet prefer to go on holiday with their friends. I've offered them free accommodation for their friends too, but they like to be independent.'

She smiled at the contradiction he presented. He might be a hard-headed businessman, but he was also still the big-hearted, family-orientated person she'd once loved.

Miranda had told her that their mother was still somewhat of a recluse after her husband had abandoned her the final time, even though it had been over eight years ago. It was a shame she was missing out on experiencing her son's accomplishments.

Instinctively, Saira reached out to give him a sympathetic pat, but her hand had a mind of its own, coming to rest on the warmth of his hard biceps.

'What?' Nathan asked, his eyes boring down at her hand.

'Oh, nothing. Sorry.' She hurriedly removed it.

Turning too quickly, to avoid the intensity in Nathan's gaze, Saira tripped and face-planted into the sand. Warm hands on her shoulder and waist gently turned her onto her side, then her back, their touch heating her skin more than the sun. She blinked as his head blocked the sun.

'Are you okay? Nothing broken?' he asked, moving her hair behind her ears.

She would swear he was trying not to laugh.

She nodded. 'Fine.' She grabbed his arms for balance as she slowly sat up rubbing her forehead. 'I'm fine.'

'You should rest for a few minutes,' Nathan said. 'I'll help you back to a sun lounger.'

Their walk had brought them close to where their friends were playing volleyball. Near them was a seating area where the afternoon tea Nathan had ordered had been laid out.

Carefully he supported her to stand. Enjoying the secure and protected sensation of his arm round her shoulder, she resisted the urge to bury herself in his chest.

After he'd set her down on a lounger, Nathan brought over some drinks and a fruit platter. 'How are you feeling?' he asked. 'Still shook up?'

She shook her head. 'I'm okay. Not too bruised, apart from my dignity.'

His mouth quirked. 'Still not an athlete, I see.'

She laughed. 'No. I must have two left feet.'

'I wouldn't say that.'

'No?' she asked, tilting her head up at him.

'I've seen you dance.'

Heat filled her cheeks as her mind burned with the memory of the last time they'd danced. It had been her second year of university. They'd been back together for a couple of months. He'd completed an important deal and wanted to celebrate with an outing to an exclusive club. The kind of place Saira would never have got the chance to go in her ordinary life.

The sensuality of the music and their movements had swept them up in a maelstrom of passion which lasted throughout their journey back to his flat, leading them almost inevitably to the bedroom, where they'd made love for the first time.

Was he remembering too?

To dispel the memories she said, 'I haven't danced in years.'

'That's a shame. There's a nightclub that's part of the hotel. It's fairly popular. We should go.'

Saira cleared her throat. That probably wasn't a good idea. 'You have great friends,' she said, to change the subject.

'I do.'

'Not many people I know are still in regular contact with uni friends,' she observed. She'd lost touch with most of her friends when she'd emigrated to the States.

'Bastien makes sure of it. And I think it's important to spend time with people if you care about them.'

For a brief moment Saira wondered whether he was thinking about his father. He'd often complained that his father hadn't spent time with them, even before his parents' divorce. But this thaw in the frost between her and Nathan was still tentative. She didn't want to risk saying anything to ruin that.

'Are you still in touch with any of your gang from school?' she asked, instead.

'Of course. Most of them.'

'How are they doing?'

Saira was soon laughing as Nathan updated her, sharing amusing anecdotes and wry observations. This man, with his teasing wit and ready smile, was the one she remembered, the man she'd fallen in love with. His relaxed countenance was a refreshing and welcome change after his previous antagonism and, worse, polite detachment.

When they'd first met he'd been only eight and she had barely registered his existence. As she grew older, and her visits to Miranda's house became less frequent because of their different schools, he had been nothing more to her than Miranda's aloof brother. It wasn't until she was sixteen and he was eighteen, when one of her friends had started going out with one of his, that she started to see him in a different light. Then she had got to spend time with him in a more casual setting, with the two groups of friends hanging out together often. In experiencing his intellect, his humour and charm first-hand, she had lost her heart.

Watching him interact with his university friends on the flight, over lunch and round the pool, she kept catching glimpses of that carefree young man from years ago. These men were good for him. They brought him out of his head and into a happier frame of mind. She suspected they had a mutual effect on each other.

She had a momentary regret for what the two of them lost as a consequence of trying to be a couple.

After he'd told her they had no future together she'd needed a clean break. Across the ocean, it had been easy enough for her to keep in contact with Miranda while cutting ties with him. Perhaps that had been a mistake. With their shared sense of humour and similar outlook on the world perhaps they were meant to be good friends.

She sighed softly. There was no point thinking about what might have been. They'd already agreed to leave the past where it belonged and concentrate on how they would act in the future.

Easier said than done when her feelings were threatening to resurface—physical feelings of attraction. Not romantic feelings. Those were definitely in the past. Romance led to heartache, and she'd had enough heartache for one lifetime.

But it was strange to be so comfortable sitting next to someone, to be relaxed in their company but at the same time intensely aware of their slightest movement. And hadn't he checked her out when they'd all been talking by the pool?

There was silence between them now.

'I've organised some jet skis,' he said, breaking the quiet. 'They should be available soon. Have you been on one before?'

She shook her head.

'Do you want to try?' he asked.

'I would love to, but it may not be the safest activity for me to risk.' She laughed self-deprecatingly.

'I'm sure you'll be fine. But if you're worried you can ride behind me.'

She took a sharp intake of breath as she imagined sitting behind Nathan, his hard body between her legs, her arms wrapped securely round his waist.

To cool her thoughts, she took a sip from her drink and winced. 'Oh, brain freeze.' She rubbed her forehead where she'd hit the sand. 'Am I going to get a bruise here?' she asked, turning her face up to his.

'I don't think so.' He brushed a kiss against her forehead. 'To make it feel better.'

Her mouth fell open. It had been the lightest of touches but her heart started pounding. She took a couple of shaky breaths, tried to speak, but couldn't get words out. If she read his wide eyes and absolute stillness correctly, he was as shocked as she was by his action.

Before either of them spoke he was hailed by his friends to join them for a volleyball game.

'Are you okay if I go?' he asked, standing.

'Of course. I'm fine now.'

She watched him as he played, every motion precise and economical, but with a caged energy. Her eyes moved from his broad shoulders to the rippling muscles displayed when he spiked the ball. The fabric of his shorts did nothing to hide his taut backside.

Her body had moved into a heightened state of arousal. So she tore her gaze away from the volleyball game and stood up. A cooling dip in the Mediterranean was needed.

Alone in their suite after dinner, Nathan poured them both a soft drink. As Housekeeping had already converted the sofa into a bed, they took their glasses out on the deck.

It had been a surprisingly good day. After their rocky start, Saira was more comfortable in his company. Their agreement to be on friendly terms for Miranda was working and they'd gradually fallen back into their old mellow ways.

There had been nothing to hint at their former romantic relationship.

Apart from his brief, impulsive kiss on her forehead earlier.

He still couldn't explain what had caused him to do that—an unwelcome throwback to their past, maybe? By silent mutual consent, neither of them acknowledged it had happened.

Dinner had been a raucous occasion, full of

laughter, when the conversation flowed easily and the topics had been diverse, causing some heated debates. Initially, as at lunch, Saira hadn't said much, but after a while she was happy to join in.

She'd been particularly eager to participate when his friends started gently ribbing him. Like theirs, Saira's teasing had been good-natured and she always took as well as she gave.

It was her teasing wit which had first drawn his attention when they were teenagers. In a large group she had never been one to make herself the centre of attention, but once he'd heard a few of her pithy observations he found himself listening out for her input, purposely drawing her into conversations when he could.

Without even trying, she'd always known exactly how to make him laugh, their sense of humour meshing perfectly.

She hadn't changed that much. Still cynical, sarcastic. Adorable.

He pressed his lips together. They'd agreed to draw a line under the past, but that would be hard to do if small actions were going to bring back memories.

Saira yawned, stretching her mouth wide. His lips quirked. She couldn't make it clearer she had no romantic interest in him. Apart from his sisters, no other woman he knew would yawn so inelegantly in front of him. But now his attention was focused on her mouth, on the tempting pout of her naturally full lips.

'I'm shattered,' she said, resting her head against the back of the seat. 'I could probably sleep for a week. But my mind is buzzing. I can't remember the last time I enjoyed dinner conversation like tonight.' Her eyes were dark and languorous. 'I know you have an early start for the dive tomorrow. Don't stay up on my account.'

He shook his head. 'It's only ten. I should probably check my emails before I go to sleep, but that can wait a few minutes. You should take the main bed tonight.' He held up a hand to stop her protests. 'It's easier for me if I work in the lounge and I don't want to disturb you.' Seeing she was still not convinced, he said, 'Or I could go to the business suite to work, if you prefer.'

She dipped her head in acknowledgement. 'If you're sure.'

He raised his eyebrows. 'That was easy.'

She twitched her nose impishly. 'I'm not going to fight too hard when someone offers me a comfy bed.'

'So your protests were only for show, then?' His lips quirked.

She shrugged.

They both smiled, their eyes meeting for a few moments before she glanced away.

Interesting. Why couldn't she maintain eye contact?

He stretched his legs in front of him, feeling more relaxed and content than he had in ages. Usually on these holidays he would work late into the night, even on the rare occasions when he brought a girlfriend with him. This time he would finalise a few details, then trust his team to deal with most issues—they could contact him if something urgent requiring his attention came up.

'Do you have any plans for tomorrow while we're diving?' he asked.

'Honestly, my plan is to do absolutely nothing while I'm here. I may book a massage or a treatment of some kind. The last few months have been quite hectic. Truth be told, even though your sister can be a steamroller sometimes, I'm grateful to her for inviting me on this holiday or I'd be rushing straight into job hunting.'

'Are you looking for an engineering job?'

'I don't know. I've only been on the outskirts of engineering work recently.'

'I can speak to Kent,' he offered. 'One of his companies is Calthorpe Engineering. His father runs it at the moment, but Kent's taking control soon, bringing it under his Calthorpe Enterprises umbrella. He may be able to help you with some leads.'

She said nothing for a few moments, her expression shuttered. Then, 'Thanks. I'll think about speaking to him.'

He narrowed his eyes. Why did he have the impression he'd offended her somehow? For every step forward they were taking, in many ways they were still on a knife-edge, and any wrong sentence could ruin the growing warmth between them.

To keep things light, he didn't delve into what caused the shift in her demeanour. 'Why do you say you've only worked on the outskirts?' he asked.

'After we got married, Dilip wanted me to work for Shah Toys—his family's company. I joined the design and production teams, and did some consumer product engineering, but the work was quite different from my electrical engineering expertise, so I took a back seat. Besides, it's not like I could come up with new product ideas myself. I can create the necessary components, but what do I know about what games children like?'

There was some sadness in her voice when she mentioned children. Part of him wanted to ask more, but he didn't want to upset her—and, if he was honest with himself, he didn't want to hear about her marriage to another man.

'Anyway, enough about work,' Saira said. 'How did you get into diving and where are your favourite spots?'

He answered her, trying to make eye contact, but she continued to avoid looking at him directly even as she asked questions. He couldn't tell whether she genuinely wanted to know about diving or if she was trying to distract herself.

Did she feel the attraction he did?

It didn't matter if she did. They couldn't act on it. Shouldn't. Nothing had changed since they'd broken up all those years ago. He still couldn't offer her a long-term commitment and she was unlikely to agree to anything less. Any attempt to rekindle their affair would risk hurting her. Hurting them both. Again.

He openly studied Saira's profile as she sat in the moonlight, the reflected light glimmering off her delicately carved facial bones. Maturity had heightened her beauty. He'd always loved her face, but it was its expressive nature and the intelligence clearly on display which captivated him, not its bone structure.

Saira sighed deeply, looking over the faint lights to the horizon, reflected in the dark waters. 'This is the most beautiful view.'

'Yes, it is,' he replied, his eyes fixed on her.

CHAPTER FOUR

THE DAY HAD passed by in a haze of blissful relaxation by the pool. Now, after dinner, Saira went to her room, sorting through the borrowed clothes on her bed, trying to choose something to wear for dancing.

Dancing!

Apparently, the hotel nightclub was quite glamorous—the smart trousers and blouse she'd worn at dinner wouldn't be up to scratch. Not that the other women in the group had said so that blatantly. But they'd been quick in offering her the spare dresses they'd brought with them.

Who even brought spare posh frocks for a five-day diving holiday?

She grimaced. She was being uncharitable. All the women were kind and generous, and now she was spoiled for choice.

She picked up one of the dresses at random to try it on.

It wasn't the outfit. It was the idea of dancing. And Nathan. Mostly Nathan.

So far she hadn't seen much of him. She'd been asleep when he'd left for diving. More accurately, she'd stayed in the bedroom until she heard him leave.

By the time the group had returned from their dive she'd been waiting with Miranda at the bar, to make sure there was no chance she would be in the bungalow alone with him. Over dinner she'd taken a seat as far away from him as she could, short of eating at a different table. She'd stared in his direction more than she would like to admit, but any time he'd caught her eye she looked away.

There was no way she could pretend he didn't know she was avoiding him.

The previous evening, although their conversation had been friendly and fairly innocuous, she'd been more than aware of a simmering sensual tension between them. Or maybe it was only on her part, and she'd imagined the intensity in the way he stared at her.

Her mouth suddenly went dry. She licked her lips. Her libido had flared back to life in the worst circumstances. But it wasn't anything serious. It was a simple bodily reaction in the presence of a handsome man. That was all it was.

She sniggered. She was doing a pretty bad job of convincing herself that was all it was. It wasn't *any* man. It was Nathan.

All the Six-Month Men were without exception gorgeous, but whenever she was near one of them—nothing. Her body remained quiet. No, her body only reacted when she was with Nathan—the man who'd broken her heart. The man who'd told her there was no future for them.

Which wasn't a problem. She wasn't looking for a future with anyone. She was looking forward to a life of independence with a fulfilling career.

'Hey, are you decent?' Nathan called out from the living room.

'Just a sec,' she called back.

She took a few calming breaths, rubbing her hands down the sides of the mini dress she'd picked out.

Act normal, she instructed herself. *He's your best friend's brother. Nothing more.*

She left the bedroom. 'Hi, Nathan. Are people waiting for me?' She faltered at his dark, intense expression as he stood staring at her. With a nervous laugh, she asked, 'What's wrong? Is there something wrong with this dress?' She performed a twirl, feeling the skirt of the dress flaring off her legs.

'That dress is perfect,' he said, swallowing. 'You look beautiful.'

Her eyes widened. Beautiful? Her heart tripped. He used to call her beautiful back when they were dating. He was probably the only person in the world who would describe her that way. Cute, pretty, maybe attractive—not beautiful. It used to fill her with happiness…she'd taken it as a sign he must have feelings for her.

She mentally rolled her eyes at her youthful naivety. She wasn't going to make that mistake again. Nathan had made it clear he didn't offer love or marriage. Calling her beautiful was a meaningless compliment which he probably used with every woman.

She decided to keep things light. 'Thank you. You scrub up quite nicely yourself.'

An understatement, of course. His pale blue shirt, open at the neck, showed off the contoured muscles of his chest. She flexed her hand. Quickly looking round, she picked up her key card, needing to hold something to stop her reaching for him.

She fumbled with her dress. 'Of course this doesn't have pockets. And I don't have an evening bag. Maybe I should change into trousers. Do I need cash or can I charge things?' She was talking too much, trying to cover her nerves. 'Oh, we never discussed how we'd sort out the charges. Presumably it will be itemised, so we can sort it out at the end. Or should I keep a tally of—?'

'Saira,' he interrupted her.

'Yes.'

'I own the place. You don't have to worry about charges.'

She frowned. 'Are the others paying for their food and drink?'

He hesitated. 'No.'

'Hmm…why don't I believe you?'

'I don't ask them to pay anything.'

'I'm sure you don't. But I can pay my own way. I'm not trying to freeload here.'

'Nobody said you are.' He raised his hand. 'Come on, the others are waiting. We can talk about this another time. I'll have my key-card, so you don't have to take yours.'

'What about if I'm ready to leave for the night and you're still having fun shaking your booty on the dance floor?' She accompanied her words with a little shimmer.

He cleared his throat. 'Shaking my booty? Yes, of course. You know me so well.'

They laughed. If they could just stay in the zone of easy-going friendship, her life would be so much easier. She suspected there was little chance of that.

Music was thumping as they were driven in a golf buggy up to the nightclub. There was a queue outside, but she followed Nathan to the side door from where they were led to a hospitality room with a large window facing the dance floor and another door leading down to it. Being in a separate room, although the music was loud, they were able to chat comfortably to the people near them.

Soon most of the group were out dancing. The only couple left besides her and Nathan were otherwise occupied. She glanced at Nathan out of the corner of her eye. Was this awkward for him too?

To break the silence, she asked him about his diving plans for the next day. He moved closer to her, bending his head as she spoke. Her breath came faster at his closeness and heat rose in her cheeks. She barely heard his answer as memories of their nights spent close together crowded her mind.

His proximity was too much. It was pointless denying she was sexually attracted to Nathan. But she needed to be independent, not starting a relationship—or restarting one. Acting on that attraction would be the worst thing she could do. Wouldn't it?

She stood up abruptly. 'I think I'll join the dancing now.'

Nathan watched Saira leave, then followed her progress through the window as she made her way to Miranda and Steve. A little rigid to begin with, she gradually relaxed and matched the rhythm of the thrumming beats. She moved with the same sensual grace he remembered from their time together.

His eyes narrowed when he saw a man move up to her, trying to get her to dance with him.

He pushed forward, ready to go to her, sitting back down when she laughingly fended off the man's advances.

He left the room, taking a vantage point on the side-lines. From there he would be in a better position to intervene if Saira, or anyone else, needed him. Rahul and Bastien joined him, trying to convince him to get on the dance floor, but he resisted, telling them he didn't usually dance—didn't usually go to nightclubs. But the real reason behind his refusal was the strength of his urge to get close to Saira, hold her, move with her.

Far safer for him to keep his distance.

He walked slowly round the nightclub, making sure Saira remained in his field of vision—in case she needed his help shaking off more unwanted attention.

He smiled as he glanced at his sister, dancing close to Steve. She looked so happy. The two of them were deeply convinced they were in love. Then his gaze moved to his friends, dancing close with their current partners. Any casual observer would also think those couples adored each other, but Nathan knew all his friends would have someone else in their arms in six months' time.

They were all honest. They weren't offering a long-term relationship. Love was an illusion and the people who believed in it only ended up getting hurt in the long run.

Instinctively, his gaze went to Saira. She did look amazing in that dress.

He joined his friends on the dance floor, deliberately positioning himself away from Saira, even avoiding having her in his eyeline.

He could admit it. He was attracted to Saira—physically. It wasn't anything to be concerned about. He'd been attracted to many women and not acted on it. He was in control of his sexual appetite. He could easily ignore this attraction.

Starting anything with Saira would be a monumentally bad idea. It would be going backwards, not forwards. She was love and marriage. He was sex and commitment-free fun. He'd been called cold, callous, heartless by previous girlfriends. He couldn't deny it. He was the way he was. And the way he was would break Saira's heart—while his would remain unaffected.

After the fourth woman had come up to him, trying to get him to dance with her, he went back to the private room. He wasn't interested in them. He wasn't desperate for sex.

A few minutes later, Saira came into the room to ask for the key-card.

'I'll come back with you,' he offered.

'You don't have to do that. Stay. Enjoy yourself.' She grinned, making him catch his breath. 'Keep shaking your booty.'

Someone sniggered.

'Stop calling it that!'

She gave him an impish grin.

He smiled back. 'Come on, let's go. We can ask the concierge to order a car back to the bungalow.'

Once outside, Saira stood staring at the lights separating the hotel grounds from the beach.

'It's so lovely here, Nathan. I'm quite hot after all that dancing. I think I'll get some fresh air before I head back. I fancy a walk along the beach.'

'All right. Give me a minute. I'll come with you.' He quickly arranged for a car to meet them at the beach restaurant, giving them a ten-minute walk.

They walked to the water's edge. Saira bent to take her sandals off.

'I love feeling sand beneath my feet,' she said with a sigh.

'I'm surprised you have the energy to walk after all that dancing,' he said, forcing himself to tear his gaze away from the slender length of her legs.

She grinned. 'It was so fun. And you. You have serious moves. I forgot.' She patted his arm.

'You attracted a lot of attention yourself,' he said.

'How do you know? Were you watching?' she asked with a laugh.

He cursed internally at what he'd inadvertently revealed. 'I saw somebody try to dance with you.'

She stood still, her frown visible in the moonlight. 'I was probably one of the only single women there tonight. Unfortunate. I may not ever want to be in a relationship again, but I don't fancy the idea of hooking up with a stranger I meet in a nightclub either.'

'You don't think you'll get married again?' he asked in surprise. She was only twenty-eight. It would be unusual for her to remain single.

'Never. All I want is to get a job and find a place to live. By myself. On my own. No marriage—not even a boyfriend.'

Nathan processed her words as they were driven back to the bungalow. Did she mean what she said? She wasn't interested in a relationship? That could change things.

He'd heard her shortness of breath, her small gasps at their slight contact on the walk and in the back of the car. There was an attraction simmering between them. He felt it. He could tell from her body's reaction she did too.

The question was whether they should act on it. Earlier he'd determined it was a bad idea. But after what she'd said, was it possible Saira would accept a brief affair—no emotions, no strings?

He would make it clear that was all that was on offer. He wouldn't make the same mistake he'd made before. They'd never properly discussed the future the last time—she'd still been studying, with a year abroad to come, and he'd been building a new business. There had been no need. But it hadn't been unreasonable for her to presume there would be long-term relationship—maybe even marriage.

After his father had left Nathan knew there was no such thing as love or happily-ever-after, and he hadn't wanted to give Saira any false expectations. A brief memory of her expression when he told her flashed before him. She'd looked...stricken?

He shook his head to clear the image. He didn't want to think about it. He didn't want to think about the past and its painful memories. He meant what he'd said their first day in Malta. He wanted to put their prior relationship behind them. If Saira could do the same—forget about the past and accept a short-term sexual relationship—then perhaps they could enjoy and explore the physical attraction shimmering between them.

It was worth taking the chance to find out.

Once back in their bungalow, Saira went straight onto the deck. She needed to get away from the intensity of Nathan's presence. At the edge of the deck she rested her hands lightly against the glass railing, desperately wanting to break the charged atmosphere between them.

She took a few steadying breaths, trying to get her thoughts in order. Her efforts were in vain when he came to stand next to her, making her pulse race.

Her mouth went dry. She swallowed.

What did he want?

The gentlest of touches against her neck, his thumb stroking her nape, caused sensations to tingle through her body, turning her breasts heavy and aching. His hand moved from her nape to her shoulder, turning her to face him, and his other arm encircled her waist.

She stared deeply into his eyes, helpless to pull away from their intensity. 'What are you doing?' she whispered.

'Can't you tell?' he replied, his head moving closer. 'I'm going to kiss you. Is that all right?'

An image flashed into her mind of them, when they were teenagers, sitting on a couch watching a movie. Did he even realise he'd used exactly the same words he'd said the first time they kissed?

She licked her lips, milliseconds before his mouth covered hers. His lips were soft, gently exploring her mouth, not urging but coaxing her response. She willingly returned the pressure, rediscovering his warmth.

It could have been seconds or minutes before she pulled away, burying her face in his neck. She didn't understand what was happening. Drugged by their kisses, she forced her mind to ignore the protests of her body and tried to think rationally.

She pressed the lightest of kisses on his neck, then pushed herself out of his arms. 'I think I need to go to bed,' she said, reaching up to run a finger along his jaw.

His hand trapped hers against his mouth planting a kiss against her palm. 'Go,' he said. 'We'll talk tomorrow.'

CHAPTER FIVE

THE NEXT DAY Saira decided to look around the main hotel rather than spend time with Miranda, lying by the tranquil marble pool in the resort spa. She didn't want to avoid her best friend—Miranda was the reason she was on this holiday in the first place, and they still had catching up to do—but until she'd worked through her own thoughts she couldn't talk about them with anyone else, and Nathan's sister was, unfortunately, the last person she could use as a sounding board.

Anyway, relaxation was unlikely while her mind kept replaying that kiss from the night before.

Was this how Sleeping Beauty felt after being awakened from her slumber by an amazing kiss?

Maybe it wasn't completely unexpected that Nathan should be the one to wake up this physical response which had lain dormant since Dilip died. Nathan was her first—her first kiss, her first sexual encounter, her first love. Dilip was her second. There had never been a third.

When she was sixteen, and had first got together with Nathan, at her insistence they'd kept their relationship a secret from everyone—her parents in particular. But there had been no excuse when she was at university.

At the time she'd justified it because Miranda had been dealing poorly with the breakup from her long-term high school boyfriend, not to mention dealing with the collapse of her parents' marriage. It would have been insensitive to flaunt their new relationship in front of her.

But if anything happened between her and Nathan now—if they *wanted* something to happen—she wasn't going to hide it from her friend. Which was an added complication. If they started something there might be unintended consequences for her friendship with Miranda. Not something she was prepared to risk.

There was clearly some sexual chemistry between them. But was it just the embers of an old flame brought back to life by their forced proximity? Or was there something new burning between them?

Although their break-up had been inevitable, perhaps she wasn't as reconciled to it as she had convinced herself. Maybe there *was* unfinished business between them. They clearly had differing views on how and why it had ended. Nathan claimed she'd run away, but to her he'd been clear he didn't believe in love or long-term, so what kind of relationship could they have had?

She'd agreed to draw a line under the past so they could be comfortable with each other when people were around. Could they maintain that decision if they gave in to their attraction?

The grounds of the hotel were breath-taking. It would take her days to explore the outside alone. She walked along the traditional Maltese limestone paths towards the sounds of laughter and splashing from one of the hotel's four pools, then walked round the perimeter towards the gardens, with their mix of Mediterranean and African flora. She looked out for the small details Nathan had mentioned, designed to support conservation and wildlife without being too intrusive in the lush surroundings.

He'd accomplished so much in such a short time frame—less than ten years since he started his company. Would he have been as successful if they had stayed together? She laughed humourlessly. There was no realistic chance they would have stayed together all these years. Their relationship had been as time-bound then as all his relationships in the intervening years.

Years ago she'd dreamed of a future with Nathan—getting married, having children, growing old together. Then he'd made it clear he didn't see their future the same way. He wasn't offering marriage or children.

The irony was if they got together now they would be on exactly the same page.

She paused, arrested by the scenario forming in her head. Perhaps she'd dismissed the idea of a fling too hastily.

She'd loved Dilip, still grieved his loss. She wasn't looking for a husband or even a relationship. She had buried her dreams of having a husband and a family when Dil died.

But she was only twenty-eight. Had she assumed she would remain celibate for the rest of her life? Was it time for her to come out of her protective bubble and live a little? Perhaps a brief time-limited fling was exactly what she needed. There was no way she could deny the physical attraction between her and Nathan. She would be able to get him out of her system once and for all.

Restarting her career and finding a place to stay was her priority, so she could finally be independent. But as a modern independent woman surely she could own her sex drive. Instead of fighting the physical attraction she could give in to it, explore it. Without worrying about emotions.

She was so used to doing what was expected of her, trying not to disappoint anyone, even hiding her relationship with Nathan in case it caused problems in her family. Now, for the first time in a long time she could do what she wanted—have some fun. A short-term affair would be a perfect symbol to remind her that she was in control of her own destiny. Having an affair with Nathan would bring them full circle.

Although in the past she'd never had sex without having romantic feelings for the person, that didn't mean she couldn't try now. And it wasn't as if she was completely detached from Nathan. She admired him more than anyone else she knew, and she could acknowledge there were some lingering feelings.

But she needed to be careful. Could she maintain a sex-only relationship with him? It would be so easy to fall for him again… Although that was unlikely when they only had three days of holiday left.

The more she thought it through, the more she was convinced. If they took this physical attraction to its logical conclusion they could keep their past relationship where it belonged and find a new way to get along for Miranda's sake. These few days on holiday would be the perfect opportunity to indulge in a brief, intense fling.

Grinning at her bold decision, she hurried back to the bunglow.

The bungalow was empty when Nathan returned from diving. There were no messages from Saira. Hopefully she wasn't avoiding him.

Her reaction to him last night proved there was still something between them. There was unfinished business, but it was physical attraction only. Saira wasn't a young girl any more. If he suggested a brief sexual relationship, she might be open to it.

He should have spoken to her before they'd kissed. He'd meant to, but he hadn't been able to resist her as she stood against the railings with the moonlight reflected in her eyes.

This afternoon, though, they would have the conversation.

He grimaced. He hoped he hadn't given her the wrong impression. He didn't want to hurt her ag—

He deliberately turned his thoughts away from examining the past too closely.

They would both have to forget about whatever had happened in the past if they wanted to indulge their physical attraction and finish this thing between them once and for all.

By the time he'd showered and changed into cargo shorts and a blue polo shirt Saira had returned. If he'd expected her to be shy or awkward after their kiss, he was wrong. Her radiant smile when she saw him caused a strange pull inside his chest.

She sat down, putting her legs underneath her. He gave her a brief account of the dive in answer to her questions, then asked, 'What about you? What have you been up to?'

'I've been having a lovely relaxing day,' she replied.

Her short sundress rode up her legs, exposing her shapely thighs as she stretched luxuriously. His gaze wandered along the length of her body. He swallowed. If everything worked out as he wanted he would be able to run his hands over the same path his eyes travelled soon, but they needed to talk first.

Cards on the table was the best policy.

'Do you have any plans now, or would you like to go for a short ride?' he asked. 'I have a beach buggy ready. There's a place I'd like to show you.'

'Sounds lovely. I'll put my bag away and be right with you.'

He drove her quickly round the main resort area, pointing out the facilities and a few areas of ecological and geographical interest, then drove the buggy to a secluded cove away from both the main hotel and the bungalows.

'This place is amazing!' she exclaimed, taking in the view of pristine white sands as she got out of the buggy. 'I didn't read about this on the website.'

'It's my personal beach. Guests aren't permitted to come here.'

He took a beach blanket, a parasol and the picnic basket prepared by his staff out of the buggy. As Saira wandered down to the water's edge he set things up on a shady area of the beach, protected from the wind.

As she turned back to him her intake of breath was noticeable, and he gazed at the scene, trying to see it from her perspective. There was an obvious intimacy in the way the parasol had been set over the blanket, made more romantic in the light cast by the lowering afternoon sun.

'Come over here and have something to eat,' he said, patting the blanket next to him.

She gave him a weak smile and said, 'This is absolutely delightful. Thank you so much for this. I'm so grateful to you for taking the time.'

Nathan's lips twitched and he bit his lip. 'You're using that voice again.'

'What do you mean? What voice?'

'The one from a Noel Coward play.'

Saira laughed at the description, relaxing slightly. She sat down on the blanket. 'I'm a little bit nervous,' she admitted, spilling some of her drink as she reached to take a glass from him. She rolled her eyes, shook her head. 'Oops!'

He smiled, taking the glass back from her. Apart from when she was doing sports, she was so poised and graceful. She looked beautiful, sitting under the parasol with the sun casting arresting shadows across her face.

He leaned over to brush his mouth against hers.

Heat flared between them, their mouths and tongues meeting in a reciprocal thrust and parry. He covered her body as she lay down, her arms encircling his shoulders, pulling him closer.

He kissed his way along her jaw to her ear, nibbling gently before continuing his path down her neck. His hand slid along her legs to her hip, skimming the soft, smooth skin of her waist, resting briefly on her stomach, before moving to the hem of her sundress.

Suddenly he became aware of their surroundings. He moved away from her, trying to get his body under control. The attraction between them had always been strong. He'd never been able to resist her. But they had to talk first. He had to make sure she understood what the situation was—make sure that they both knew where they stood.

'Why is this happening?' she asked as she sat up.

He lay back on the blanket. 'It's simple. We're still attracted to each other,' he replied.

She nodded. 'Yes. But sex was never the problem between us.'

His body reacted under the intensity of her gaze as it travelled along his hips and chest to his face. Their eyes met, heat immediately flaring between them again.

'No, it wasn't.' There was no denying that physically they had always been in tune.

They were silent for a few moments.

'So, what do you want to do?' she asked.

'What do you mean?'

'What were you thinking would happen between us now?'

He sat up and reached out for her hand. 'You know I'm attracted to you. I want to make love with you. But I'm not going to lie and say we're together for ever from now on. I'm not offering anything more than a brief affair. I may hate being called a Six-Month Man, but it's true. I don't do long term. I don't do marriage. Even six months is probably stretching it. But I won't offer anything more. I don't want any false expectations.'

She blinked. 'So I shouldn't bother buying any bridal magazines? Well, thank you for being so frank.'

'I've learnt it's the best way,' he replied, ignoring her sarcasm. 'I don't want anyone claiming I led them on. Nobody gets hurt.'

The worst situation was when someone believed they had fallen in love with him. He usually made sure he got out before that could happen.

'Oh, don't worry. I think you've made it quite clear, on a number of occasions, there is no future here. I'm under no illusions about that.'

She pulled her hands away, hugging her legs to her chest and resting her chin on her knees.

He narrowed his eyes. Where was this bitterness coming from? Was she talking about the past? It didn't matter. It was pointless going down that path. They needed to agree on whether they would have a brief affair now—not discuss what had happened before.

He frowned. Would she expect them to rehash their past before they had an affair? It wasn't something he was prepared to do.

'I'm not going to seduce you,' he said. 'If you are happy to see where this attraction goes, that's great. If you prefer not to then that's what it is. I want to be clear up front that all I'm offering is a brief affair.'

She was silent a few moments, then she nodded. 'You're right. I'm sorry. It's good to set out the limitations from the beginning so we don't have any expectations. Like I said last night, I don't want a relationship. I'm not looking for love or romance. But I'm only twenty-eight. I don't have to be celibate for the rest of my life. I'm in control of my sex life.'

She sounded as if she was convincing herself. But if thinking out loud was helping her decide to agree to their affair he wasn't going to interrupt.

'And you're the best person to have a fling with,' she continued. 'You'll have no expectations from me either. All you want is sex. And that's all I want too.'

They were exactly the words he wanted to hear. So why was there a sensation in his chest as if he'd lost something special?

'And what's a sun and sea holiday without sex?' she asked with a laugh.

Nathan tilted his head. He hadn't thought about how long their affair would last. He was offering her a brief affair, but he hadn't quantified what 'brief' would be—he was happy to let their relationship run its course. Because all his relationships naturally ended after a few weeks or months. Either he got bored or he began to suspect the woman was developing feelings for him. That could be the only reason he hadn't thought about an end date with Saira. But perhaps limiting the duration was something to consider.

'Do you want this to be a holiday fling? Does setting an end date make a difference?' he asked.

'It does. I never liked lying to Miranda about us. But I'm not sure if she'll understand this is just a fling. She'll probably think we're a couple, and then there's the worry we'd end the affair in a bad way, which would complicate the wedding plans.' She laughed. 'I mean, Nathan, the whole point of us drawing a line under the past is so we can get along for Miranda's sake. I think we need to agree to an end date now.'

He frowned as various scenarios went through his mind. She was right. There was a risk they could ruin any prospect of a cordial relationship in the future by indulging in an open-ended affair. It wouldn't be a problem for him. Sex was sex. It didn't matter whether he slept with someone once or thirty times—he never got emotionally involved. He wasn't capable of those big all-encompassing emotions like love. His heart was quite safe. He made sure of that.

Was Saira's? She claimed to be open to a sexual fling, but she was a loving person. Even though she'd left him behind without a backward glance all those years ago, he knew she'd cared about him then. There was a risk she would start to care about him again, want more from him than he would give. He couldn't take that chance.

Perhaps starting anything with Saira was a bad idea, given their history. Unless… Unless they agreed from the outset that their affair would end with the holiday. That way there would be no need for them to discuss the past at all.

He smiled, reaching out for her hand, running his thumb across her palm. The sharp intake of her breath confirmed his thoughts. Their attraction was strong. Better to keep their fling short and sweet. For her sake.

'I agree we should set an end date,' he said.

His eyes gazed down the length of her body. Three nights was short, but he had no doubt the time they had would be amazing.

He waggled his eyebrows in an exaggerated gesture. 'But aren't you worried? We're only here for a few days. You may not be ready for the sex to end so soon.'

'I don't know...' she teased with a wink. 'I don't remember the sex being that good.'

'I'm happy to give you a reminder.'

They'd gone from serious to light-hearted so quickly. With anyone else he would have found the changing moods frustrating, but he enjoyed Saira's unpredictability. It kept it him on his toes. He found it challenging rather than irritating.

'All right,' she said quickly.

'All right, what?'

'All right, a brief affair or fling while we're on holiday. Then we're back to real life and you're only my best friend's older brother. That works for me. Let's do it,' she said, groaning as he laughed at her unintentional double entendre.

His laughter faded as they stared at each other. She started to move her head but he cupped her chin, turning her towards him, running his hand along the soft, warm skin of her forehead, down her temple, gently moving strands of hair behind her ear before cupping her cheek, caressing her open lips with his thumb, feeling her breath warm against its tip.

He leaned in, replacing his hand with his mouth. She reached up to cup his neck, bringing him closer. Moments later he pulled back.

He didn't want to make love to her on the beach. It sounded romantic, but the sand was probably uncomfortable.

'Hold that thought,' he said with a shaky breath.

Her forehead crinkled with confusion.

'Later,' he promised.

'Later,' she repeated, nodding.

She gazed out across the sea, a variety of emotions playing over her face. Then she turned to him with a wide smile.

'So what's in the picnic basket?' she asked.

The sofa bed wasn't made up when Saira entered the suite after dinner. She gulped. She was glad Nathan wasn't with her. Could he have told Housekeeping not to bother? That would have been an interesting conversation.

It was awkward, obsessing over what would happen next. Should she get into bed and lie there waiting for him? She'd never had an affair before. Was there an accepted etiquette for this situation?

Too wound up even to think about going to bed now, she walked out onto the deck. Would it be pure indulgence if she turned on the sunken hot tub? She checked her watch. It was only ten. She didn't know how long Nathan would be. He was enjoying a game of pool with the other Six-

Month Men—it would have been too obvious if he'd been the only one of them to turn down a game.

She decided to change into her bikini, then enjoy a glass of wine while soaking in the hot tub, taking in the view of the starlight reflected in the Mediterranean.

Moments later, refusing to think any more about the future, Saira laid her head back, closing her eyes to indulge in the sensations as the bubbles gently burst around her. Whether it was the balmy night air against her heated cheeks or the soothing warm water lapping against her sensitive skin, images flooded through her mind of the times she and Nathan had made love in the past, making her whole body tingle and her breath come faster.

She didn't know how long it had been before her eyes opened as she heard a sharp exhalation.

Nathan stood on the deck, boldly staring at her as she lay in the water. Every nerve-ending fired into life under his intense scrutiny. She gulped, trying to take in the oxygen that had deserted her, her breasts heavy with anticipation.

As Nathan stalked towards her she slowly climbed out of the hot tub, neither of them breaking eye contact. He bent to capture her lips, one strong hand cradling her neck, angling her head for better access, while he ran warm, sensuous caresses along her spine to her rear.

The cool night air against her damp body was warmed by his strong persuasive hands, combining to cast a seductive spell she had no power to resist. As the ground moved from beneath her she instinctively wrapped her legs around his waist. He carried her as far as the outdoor seating area before sitting down with her straddling him.

'I'm getting your clothes wet,' she said, in between deep, intoxicating kisses.

'Help me out of them,' he said, leading her hands to his shirt buttons.

He kissed along her neck as her fingers explored more of his skin with every button she undid. She leaned back to enjoy the sight of his broad chest, unable to resist the urge to let her lips and tongue follow where her hands had led.

With a groan, Nathan ran his fingers through her hair, stopping her exploration so he could bring her mouth back to his. His thumbpad flicked over her hardened nipple, causing her a momentary recollection that her bikini top had been removed.

Her hands were reaching for his waistband when he covered them.

'Wait,' he gasped.

She growled. 'Please don't ask me to hold this thought again.'

'No.' He spoke in between more kisses. 'But I don't have any protection here.'

'What? At the resort?'

'Out here. But there's some in the bedroom.'

She sat back, panting, taking in their half-naked bodies. 'Let's go, then.'

CHAPTER SIX

IT HAD BEEN over a month since Saira had returned to London—the weeks had flown by.

Her short holiday had been perfect. She'd spent her days catching up with Miranda—loving the chance to reconnect with her best friend—and the evenings had usually been spent as a group, eating and chatting. But the nights had been filled with Nathan. With intoxicating kisses, long, languid explorations of each other's bodies, and deep, passionate lovemaking.

After they'd returned from Gozo they initially stuck to their decision to end the fling. A week later she had met Miranda and Steve at a bar. Nathan joined them. He offered to see her home. She invited him in for a drink.

He'd left the next morning.

They hadn't discussed what this continued affair meant. They should have been sensible and set an end date. She hadn't exactly signed up to this modern, short-term, no expectations relationship. Not that it *was* a relationship. More a series of one-night stands.

Which suited her perfectly. She didn't want any kind of real relationship. Her future didn't have to be lonely, but she didn't need a man around to make her life complete.

Their fling would end sooner or later. The only reason it hadn't yet was because they were both so busy they hardly got a chance to see each other.

Her days were filled with job hunting and flat hunting. She was ready to move out of the hotel and into a place of her own. Not that she had any complaints with the place Nathan organised for her. Far from it. She'd been expecting a standard room, but he'd arranged for her to have one of the best suites. Only the Royal and Presidential Suites in the hotel were more magnificent.

She would never get used to the breath-taking views of Green Park from her living room, or to opening her bedroom curtains to see Buckingham Palace. There was also a separate dining room, kitchenette, study and second bedroom. It was the most opulent setting she ever experienced, even after the luxury of the Haynes Malta Beach Resort.

Her lips twitched as she recalled his response to her offer to pay for the suite, when he'd quoted from Chapter Seventeen of the *Bhagavad Gita* on gift-giving without expectation at the right time in the right place to the right person, using her own words against her.

Sometimes, though, she wanted more than meals out or hotel food, no matter its Michelin star quality. The kitchenette was fine for preparing simple dishes and snacks, but designed primarily for caterers to warm meals—she couldn't cook from scratch in it. So she'd started going to her parents' flat to cook proper meals.

Saira kicked off her shoes and took the curry she'd made that afternoon at her parents' into the kitchen. She would have a long soak in the bath, followed by dinner with a movie.

Her phone pinged while she was putting the food into the fridge.

I have theatre tickets for tonight. The theatre's in Victoria. The car will collect you at six pm.

She shook her head at Nathan's text. They hadn't discussed getting together that evening. Did he expect her to be available at his whim?

In many ways it was like when she'd been at university, only back then half his texts had been cancelling on her. This time *she* would be the one changing plans. Not that it even was a plan, when it had been arranged last minute with no input from her.

She texted back.

Sorry, I'm staying in tonight. Hope the ticket doesn't go to waste.

If her days were busy, her social life was more hectic than it had ever been. On the evenings she wasn't with Nathan she was spending time with Miranda, or with her older brother Ajay, his wife and children. Occasionally she met up with people she'd lost touch with when she'd lived in the States.

With Nathan travelling a lot for work, they only had a few opportunities during the week to see each other. And when she and Nathan did get together he always wanted to be out doing something—going out for dinner, to the cinema, to plays or the opera. Always places where other people were around. It was as if the only time he could be alone with her was when they were in bed.

Spending time with Nathan in bed was always wonderful. Whether their lovemaking was soft and slow, or hard and fast, or anything in between, their bodies were perfectly in tune. So why was she not content?

Because she missed talking with Nathan—missed the old certainty that their minds were as attuned as their bodies. They didn't talk about anything deep or meaningful now. Although drawing a line under the past had been a good plan for their getting on for the sake of Miranda, or even indulging in a holiday fling, it would be hard to avoid mentioning their former relationship if they did start having proper conversations.

Until they discussed what had happened between them before she'd left for the States there would never be closure enough for them to have a future together.

She rolled her eyes. There *was* no future for them. Nathan had been clear eight years ago, and again when they were in Malta. And it was the same for her. She hadn't changed her mind. Being independent was still her priority. She didn't want a future with Nathan or anyone else.

She had to stop wondering what might have been and accept the reality she was in. Stop caring. Stop developing emotions. Steel her heart. That way she would never have to experience the pain of loss again.

With a sigh, she went to run her bath, poured herself a glass of wine, then chose a book to read while she soaked.

She was warming her curry bowl in the microwave when the bell rang. She frowned. The butler hadn't phoned to announce he was attending or sending anyone up to her suite. She glanced down at the polar-bear-covered flannel pyjamas she'd changed into after her bath and shrugged.

She was comfortable and couldn't be bothered to change to answer the door.

Her eyes widened when the peephole showed Nathan standing outside. 'Didn't you get my text?' she asked as she opened the door.

Instead of replying straight away he glued his eyes to her pyjamas. 'Cute,' he said, bending to kiss her cheek. 'Yes, I got your text. Is everything okay?'

'Fine.' She walked back to the kitchen as the microwave dinged. 'Come in. I'm just about to have dinner.'

He stood near the kitchen door sniffing the aromas. 'Smells wonderful. What is it?'

'Chicken curry and saag aloo with rice.'

'From the restaurant? Or did you order a takeaway?'

'I made it.'

'You? Really?'

'Don't sound so surprised. I can cook.'

'Hmm…this I have to see. I haven't eaten yet. Is there enough for me? I could order room service if not.'

'There's enough for you, but what about the play?'

'I had my assistant return the tickets. Which reminds me…' He reached into his pocket and pulled out an envelope. 'I managed to get tickets for that Shakespeare play you mentioned.'

'The Indian adaptation of *The Tempest*?'

Saira stared at the hand holding out the ticket. She couldn't believe he'd gone to so much trouble. She'd mentioned the play in passing, as something she would have loved to watch, but performances had been sold out for months. It wasn't only his kindness and generosity in getting hold of the tickets, but also his thoughtfulness in remembering her throwaway comment. Could it mean he cared?

'Are you sure there's nothing wrong?'

Nathan's voice interrupted her thoughts. She shook her head and gave him a quick smile. 'Oh, sorry. There's nothing wrong. I'm tired and fancied a night in. I'm going to eat and watch a film.'

'All right,' he said. 'That sounds good.'

She watched as he took off his jacket and tie, then loosened the top button of his shirt. She wasn't sure about this. Only moments before she'd been complaining to herself about them always going out, but the alternative of them spending the evening in together was almost too intimate…too much like normal couple behaviour.

'Saira?'

'Sorry, what?'

'I asked if you want something to drink?'

'I already have some wine on the go. Would you like a glass?'

He efficiently prepared trays with cutlery and drinks while she plated up their meals.

'Are you sure this is okay? You don't have to stay here because I want a night at home. I don't mind if you want to leave.'

He smiled. 'And miss out on this food? Not a chance. Come on, let's watch.'

The sounds of pleasure he made as he ate were gratifying. Something about him eating a meal she'd cooked made her wish again for the kind of relationship which wasn't on offer.

She pressed play on the remote.

'Wait a minute,' he said when the film began.

'What?'

'Are you making me watch a romcom?'

'Hey! Part of the deal of you eating my food is you don't get to comment on my film choices.'

'Fine.' He grinned. 'At least the food is delicious. If I'd known you could cook like this I would have hired you for one of my restaurants.'

She rolled her eyes. 'You couldn't afford me. Now, shush, I need to concentrate.'

They ate in companionable silence. When they'd finished she scooched back to lean against the sofa, slipping off her slippers and curling her legs under her. Nathan carried the trays back to the kitchen, then returned to sit next to her, putting his arm round her shoulders. She lifted her face up to his and he dropped a kiss on her mouth, then they turned back to watch the film.

At the end of the film Saira stretched, a huge smile across her face—which faltered slightly when she met Nathan's gaze.

'What?' she asked.

'Nothing,' he replied with a shake of his head and a small smile.

Saira rolled her eyes but didn't say anything. In the past she'd often caught him looking at her rather than at the film. He'd said he loved watching her reactions as she watched.

She frowned. She should have realised memories of their time together would surface if they did the same activities. It was a big mistake, spending the evening in with Nathan. Far safer to be out on dates where there was inevitably a distance. He'd had the right idea all along.

She glanced at the time. 'It's half-nine—I suppose you have to leave now? Busy day tomorrow.'

'No, I don't have to rush,' he replied, resting his hands behind his head and leaning back. 'My first meeting tomorrow is near here. There's a documentary I'd like to watch. Do you mind?'

She shrugged, then handed him the remote control.

Nathan flipped through the channels. 'Ah, here it is,' he said.

He stretched out his legs on the footstool, then patted his lap—his old signal for her to place her legs over his as they curled up together to watch the screen.

Her breath caught. This was too much. Too evocative of their past.

Frustrated with herself for being overly emotional and contradictory, she gave herself a stern talking-to. She needed to keep their relationship strictly sexual. It was a bad idea to revive old feelings that were supposed to be dead and buried.

They'd been together only a few weeks. She didn't know how long it would be before he became tired of her and it didn't matter. Any amount of time was long enough to run the risk of her feelings growing deeper. Emotions were already surfacing. Maybe the sensible step would be to end this now.

But he had bought tickets for the play she really wanted to see, which was only a month away. It would be rude to end things before then. And the sex was great. And, overall, she was enjoying her time with him.

It was only another month. A month would go by in a flash, and they'd probably only see each other once or twice in that time. What harm could come from that?

She would be fine as long as she kept reminding herself this was a short-term sex-only thing. She was sensible—she would make sure she didn't develop deeper feelings for him. She wouldn't get hurt—not this time.

She been hurt so many times already, and experienced so much loss with Dilip's death, and then her—

She mentally shook her head. She didn't think about what had happened before. She only knew she couldn't put herself through more of that.

Nathan had the capacity to hurt her more than anyone. It had broken her heart when he'd ended things all those years ago. It had taken her a long time to move on. She had to protect herself from any future pain.

Now she was aware of the danger signs, she would proceed with caution.

Two weeks later Nathan stood in his kitchen, rinsing plates and putting them in the dishwasher. He frowned as Saira walked towards him, carrying the last of the serving dishes.

Usually he went to great lengths to avoid scenes of domesticity. His preference was to keep his relationships on a superficial level, and cooking meals together was sure to send the wrong message.

Many of his previous girlfriends had offered to cook a meal for him. He'd never accepted. It was usually a sign for him to end the relationship before they started to take things seriously. He never offered to cook for his girlfriends—never invited them to his place.

He pressed his lips together. Was he sending Saira the wrong message? Hopefully she would understand his invitation wasn't anything special. His offer to cook was a way of thanking her for sharing her curry. Nothing more.

This sense of belonging, of being perfectly comfortable with her presence, wasn't unusual when he thought about it. Saira and Miranda had often baked goodies in the kitchen when they were young. It was a throwback to those times. That was all. He often forgot how long he'd known Saira. Their aborted attempts at trying a relationship sometimes made him think that was all their history together. Part of their history he had no intention of recalling.

It had clearly been a mistake to invite her. She would probably read too much into the situation. Women inevitably did.

Staying in to make dinner for her was an aberration—like watching a film in her suite had been. The media might call him a Six-Month Man, but six months sounded like a life sentence. He preferred women who were looking for some company, an entertaining evening and good sex.

He made it crystal-clear that was all he offered. He wasn't cut out for relationships.

Saira might have initially agreed to a physical fling, but she was a romantic at heart—a relationship person. At some point she would start thinking he'd change his mind and offer her a commitment of some sort. Offer her his heart. He would never—*could* never—do that. There was still no future for them.

It wasn't in him to love, or even to offer her long term. He knew his own limitations. Better to break it off before that happened. That way nobody got hurt. If by ending a relationship sooner rather than later he could prevent someone going through the emotional pain his mother had gone through when the man she loved walked out on her, it was worth the 'Six-Month Man' reputation.

The last thing he wanted to do was hurt Saira. He did care about her. She was his sister's best friend. She would always be part of his life. But he had to make sure she understood that from his perspective nothing had changed, and spending time cooking for her didn't mean anything.

'What?' she asked, breaking into his thoughts.

He shrugged.

'You're staring at me,' she said.

'I like looking at you. That shouldn't come as a surprise.' It was good to remind her their time together was about physical attraction.

She fluttered her eyelashes. 'Why, thank you, sir. You're not so bad yourself.'

He grabbed her, lifting her onto the counter, running his hands along her legs, slipping them under her skirt. She cradled his hips between her legs.

Their kiss was interrupted by the beep of Saira's phone. He protested when she pushed him away.

As she slid onto the floor she murmured, 'Lovely, but sex on a kitchen counter probably isn't hygienic anyway.' She read her text message. 'It's Miranda,' she said. 'She's invited us for a meal with her and Steve.'

'I see,' he said in a cold tone.

They might be on the same page about having a brief fling, but there was a risk that Miranda was reading more into the situation. When they'd continued their affair in London, Saira had insisted she couldn't hide it from Miranda. She'd told her they were having a fling, but neither of them believed Miranda would accept that explanation.

Saira frowned as she sent off a text.

'What did you say?' Nathan asked. Her reply would be a good barometer of whether she had started thinking there was more to their affair.

'I said I'm happy to meet her and Steve, but dinner with the four of us isn't going to happen.'

Nathan's phone beeped. 'It's Miranda—asking why I won't go to dinner with you.' He rolled his eyes.

Saira laughed. 'I love your sister, but she needs to learn she won't get her own way all the time.'

'I suppose we *could* go to dinner. I've been to dinner with couples before.'

Usually on a first or second date, when there was still uncertainty about whether there would be enough conversation to last the evening. He was acting out of character this evening—was it their shared history confusing things?

'Not sure it's a good idea,' Saira said, walking out of the kitchen and putting her phone in her handbag. 'We're not a real couple. I don't want Miranda getting the wrong impression. She's already convinced I won't be able to separate my emotions from sex.'

She rolled her eyes, suggesting the idea was ludicrous.

Saira's confirmation she still viewed their relationship as only physical should have made him happy—he wouldn't hurt her when he ended it. So why was there a twinge of disappointment instead? It wasn't because *he'd* started to think there might be something more lasting between them, was it? No, that couldn't be it. He still couldn't offer a long-term commitment to anyone—not even Saira.

He gave her a curious look as she grabbed her jacket. 'Are you leaving?'

'I thought so. Unless you want to watch a film or documentary?'

He pressed his lips together. That would be a very bad idea. This evening had already been enough to show that his fling with Saira was a delicate balancing act between enjoying a short-term sexual relationship and the constant reminder she was already, and would continue to be, a part of his life.

He cared about her and she cared about him. Those feelings would continue to develop. On her part, at least. He would be safe. He wouldn't allow himself to have deeper feelings. *Allow* himself? This wasn't a choice. Was it?

Perhaps the best thing would be to end their affair immediately. Right then. Christmas was coming up quickly. He didn't want his family and Saira to become more enmeshed, which was bound to happen if their affair continued until then.

He gaze homed in on her body as she bent over to pick up her handbag. He swallowed.

Christmas was still several weeks away. There was time to end things before then. But for now he would get the affair back to its purely physical footing.

He walked towards her, taking her bag from her arm as he pressed light kisses on her cheek, then down and along her neck, quickly inflaming them both. All thoughts of dinners and home cooking and domesticity were forgotten as they gave in to their growing passion.

Much later that evening, Nathan raised his head as Saira climbed off him. He had a large comfortable bed only a few metres away, and instead they'd made love on his sofa. If they hadn't been interrupted earlier they would probably have made love on his kitchen counter.

Their sexual attraction was as strong as ever and showed no signs of diminishing. With others he started getting bored after the first couple of weeks, and he had assumed his sex drive was easily satisfied. With Saira he was almost insatiable.

It wouldn't last. It never did. This was nothing to worry about. The sex was great—for now. Soon the rush, the immediate reaction of his body, would fade.

Saira stood up to put her panties on, smoothing down her skirt and searching for the rest of her clothes.

'What are you doing?' he asked, lying back with his arm behind his head. His hand came across her bra and he held it out silently, a broad smile on his face.

'Getting dressed.'

'Why?'

'Because I don't want to get arrested going home half-naked,' she replied with a laugh.

'You don't have to go home. You can stay over.'

Nathan sat up.

He was breaking his own rules.

He never asked someone to spend the night with him at his place—at least not since he and Saira had dated when she was at university. That was it. Again it was their past that was the explanation for his offer. He'd momentarily had a sentimental flashback.

He needed to cut it out—stop confusing the past and their current situation.

Saira scrunched up her face. 'I'm not sure. I didn't bring anything with me.'

'Why don't I call a car for you? One of our drivers is always available,' he offered.

She threw him a surprised glance. Had she expected him to try to persuade her to stay? He had to be careful about giving her mixed signals.

He purposefully checked work emails while they waited for the car to arrive. He wanted to make sure she received the message that sex was all he wanted.

He expelled a long breath after she'd left. He'd made the right decision. He would end things before Christmas.

But she was his sister's best friend. He felt a responsibility to make sure she would be all right. He'd already sorted out accommodation for her—he didn't need to worry about that. But if she had financial security he would feel better. Perhaps he could help with her job hunt. Then he would be able to end things once and for all.

CHAPTER SEVEN

A FEW WEEKS later Saira was sitting in Nathan's chauffeur-driven car resting her head against the seat, her eyes closed as she let the breeze from the partially open window refresh her.

They had initially met at the theatre, but she'd felt faint during the interval. When she admitted she hadn't eaten much, Nathan immediately suggested they leave to get her something to eat.

It was a shame to miss the play but, in reality, she hadn't been able to concentrate anyway—too busy thinking through what she'd found out that morning, mentally rehearsing what she was planning to say to Nathan once they were in private.

She frowned when the car pulled up in front of his apartment building, where they took the private lift to his penthouse flat.

'You said you were taking me home,' she said once they were inside his place.

'This is my home. It made more sense to bring you here. Now you've moved out of the hotel, there won't be anyone to check on you if you're unwell.'

She huffed. He'd made it clear he wasn't pleased she'd moved into her own flat. But what did he expect? She wanted to be independent—which was hard to do if you were living for free in accommodation provided by your sex partner.

'It was easier to arrange for food to be delivered here. Banks took it in,' he said, referring to the building's concierge. 'He said he'd put it in the oven to keep warm.' He walked towards the kitchen. 'Ah, yes. Here it is. Are you happy to eat at the breakfast bar or shall I set the table in the dining area?'

'Kitchen is fine.'

Even though the spicy aromas from the Mexican cuisine were enticing, Saira's stomach roiled. It was probably nervous agitation, or even indignation. Her shoulders slumped as she watched Nathan take out the food.

'I'm not hungry.'

'You said you haven't eaten all day. It's not good for you. Come on, take a few mouthfuls.'

If only his concern meant something. But it didn't. Concern didn't mean caring. And what he'd done about her job wasn't about caring.

'Nathan, I'm not a child,' she bit out. 'If I don't want to eat I'm not going to eat. You can't bully me into doing something I don't want to do.'

His eyes went wide. 'I'm not trying to bully

you into anything. What *is* going on with you? You've been in a strange mood all evening.'

She ran her hands across her face. There was nothing to be gained from putting the conversation off. Nathan's natural inclination was to take charge and arrange things to his satisfaction. He acted the same way in business as he did in his home life. His mother and sisters relied on him to such an extent he felt as responsible for them as he did for his employees.

Well, she wasn't one of his employees.

'Now you mention it,' she began, 'an interesting thing did happen today. I told you I had an interview at Calthorpe Engineering's Birmingham location?' He nodded. 'Well, today their head of HR called, inviting me for a second interview. She asked if I would be interested in working in their London office instead.'

'Congratulations. That's good news, isn't it?'

'Sure. Only I never wanted to work in their London branch.'

He couldn't meet her eyes—a sure sign of his guilt.

'You spoke to Kent about me, didn't you?' she challenged.

He sighed. 'I mentioned your interview in passing. I may have said it would be easier if you could work in London since Miranda will need you close to help with wedding arrangements and so you can be near your family.'

'Be near my family?' she repeated. 'Are you serious?' She made no effort to keep the biting sarcasm from her tone.

'Yes. What's your issue? Kent didn't know about your application beforehand. I didn't ask him to offer. He's opposed to any indication of nepotism. He wasn't doing me a favour.'

'You had no right to discuss my job with Kent at all. The London office doesn't do the kind of engineering work I'm looking for. If I wanted to work there, I would have applied.' She took a couple of calming breaths. 'I can't believe you. This is my career you're interfering with.'

She had to make him understand what he'd tried to do was wrong. She wanted to be in charge of her life. She needed to be. When Nathan tried to interfere with that, he was taking away her control.

'It's not interfering.' His face was stone, his voice cold. 'I had a conversation with a friend. Nothing more. Now you have another option. Why are you making such a fuss about this?'

'Seriously?' she asked with a laugh. 'I can make my own decisions. I don't need you trying to control me.'

His lips thinned, and if possible his face hardened even more. 'I'm not trying to control you.'

She sighed. He didn't even recognise he was doing it.

'If you want to move to Birmingham, then move,' he continued. 'It's your choice.'

She nodded. 'I know it's my choice.'

Where she worked was one thing she could and would control. She had to make her own decisions, without any external inference. All her life she'd allowed people to make decisions for her—her parents, her brothers, Dilip. Even Nathan had made the decision that there wasn't any future for them. But no more.

She didn't want or need any help. She needed to show Nathan, make him realise she was independent and capable of standing on her two feet—making her own way.

'Remember that before you speak to any other friends about my career,' she warned him.

'Of course,' he said, shrugging.

She was sure he would be rolling his eyes if he didn't know it would inflame the situation. She sighed. At face value Nathan probably didn't think it was a big deal. He was acting out of kindness and trying to be helpful. He looked out for his family all the time—it was second nature to him. Had she overreacted?

She looked closely at him but couldn't interpret his expression. The silence was slightly unnerving. To break the tension, she began to eat. A delighted moan broke from her as the delicious spices fired her taste buds. Suddenly her appetite returned with a vengeance, and she'd finished her plate before Nathan spoke again.

'At the risk of having my head bitten off, can I ask how the job hunt is going?'

'I have a second video interview with a company near Chicago. It's probably the best job in terms of challenge and prospects. Keep your fingers crossed.'

'I didn't realise you were applying in the States too,' he said.

She nodded cheerfully. 'Mmm-hmm. I wasn't going to, but the job market there is much better. It doesn't make sense to limit myself geographically.'

'I see.' He stood watching her for a few moments, his eyebrows furrowed.

'What now?' she asked with an annoyed sigh.

'I was thinking of Miranda. I thought you were going to be around to support her with her wedding plans. She needs her best friend now. I would expect you to realise that.'

She bristled at the implied criticism. 'I spoke to Miranda. You know she would never stand in the way of my career or what would make me happy. International communication and travel are so easy nowadays. Besides,' she added with a small smile, 'I'm sure you'd send your jet for me if there was an emergency.'

His face remained impassive.

'What?' she bit out. 'Are you going to contact

the Chicago company to see whether they can offer me a job here?'

'For the last time: I don't care where you work. If Miranda's happy that's all that matters. Whether you decide to move to Birmingham or Chicago or anywhere else in the world is of no concern to me. I don't care where you live.'

Saira had forgotten how it felt to have her heart lacerated. He'd spoken the words so casually, not even thinking for a moment of their significance, not realising she still secretly harboured a dream which had disappeared in that moment.

Of course he had no interest in where she worked or lived in the future. Their relationship was time-limited. It had already overrun its course. How had she allowed herself to believe things could be different?

Despite her intentions, her warnings, her logical rationalisations, she much suspected she had feelings for him. If she was beginning to care for him so much after only a couple of months, the pain when he finally ended things would be devastating. She didn't want to go through that. Not again.

She had to end their fling—go back to her original plan to stay single and independent. She had to end it before her feelings could grow any deeper. End it before she could get hurt again.

She glanced over at Nathan, drinking in his

features. Her pulse sped up and her breath became shallow under his penetrating gaze.

One night to say goodbye. She could allow herself one more night.

Nathan woke as sunlight streamed onto the bed. The only problem with automated curtains was they didn't take into account when you wanted darkness to stay cocooned in bed with your girl-friend.

He turned his head, noticing Saira was also stirring. He frowned. She'd been acting unlike herself the previous evening. She said she accepted he wasn't trying to interfere with where she worked but at the same time she was distant—there was almost a forced lightness.

He wasn't trying to control her. He was trying to help her out. What was wrong with helping someone you cared about?

Cared? The word struck at him. He did care about Saira. He was bound to have some affection for her when she'd been part of his life for years. But it wasn't in the romantic sense. He didn't do those kinds of feelings. It wasn't a road he was prepared to travel down again.

Again?

He was distracted from what that implied by Saira's hand running along his chest and down to his hip. He halted her exploration, covering her body with his...

Afterwards, he rested his head on her chest.

'This is such a comfortable bed,' she said, stretching like a contented cat. 'I don't know how you ever leave it.'

'Neither do I at this moment.'

Saira laughed stroking his hair. 'You're not usually such a flirt.'

He made a sound of pleasure, pressing a kiss to her breast. He lay next to her in quiet contentment.

'Why six months?' she asked, moments later.

'What?' He went still, the question catching him off guard.

'Why Six-Month Men? Why not three months? Why not a year?'

Why was she bringing this up now? What bearing could it have? Was her interest in the longevity of his relationships something he should worry about? Was she hinting that she was hoping for something longer term?

Maybe that wasn't out of the question with Saira. He enjoyed spending time with her…he could relax in her company. But he still wouldn't offer her love or marriage.

He turned onto his back.

'Six months is something the tabloids came up with once they noticed the five of us at Bastien's Spring Ball, and six months later there were photographs of us on holiday,' he replied, choosing his words carefully.

'The tabloids?' She pressed her lips together, jutting her chin out, making her scepticism clear. 'Sure.'

'There's no actual calendar. I don't look at the date and say, *Sorry, your six months is up*,' he said, unable to disguise the annoyance in his tone.

'But it's not like you don't have form.'

'Form?' He sat up, folding his arms. 'Because I have a different partner when the media sees me at two different events in a year you think I have *form*?'

She closed her eyes and took a few breaths. 'I meant it was the same with me. Back when I was at uni we'd been together around six months when you started losing interest.'

He opened his eyes wide, not believing she could make that accusation. '*I* lost interest? I think that was you. One minute we were together and the next minute you'd run away to America.'

'You said that before,' she said in a puzzled tone.

She was also sitting up now, pulling the bed covers over her chest. Almost in unison, they moved along the bed, further away from each other.

'But I was always going to America. It was the third year of my course. You knew that.'

'I did know, but you didn't say goodbye. I thought we were doing good, and suddenly you were making excuses not to meet, or you didn't answer my calls or texts at all.'

There was a reason he didn't want to rehash their past. There was no way it could end well. Their previous relationship and the way it had ended was too closely tied up with thoughts of his father. One minute he was looking after his mother and sisters, after his father abandoned them. Then, within a few weeks, Saira had left him too. He couldn't think about one without the other.

'It was you who was never around,' Saira protested.

He rubbed his hands over his face. Regardless of his feelings, the moment of reckoning had arrived.

He shook his head. 'Never around? I spent as much time as I could with you.'

'Sure. Every spare moment you had between looking after your family and building up your business,' she replied, sarcasm dripping from her words.

'Do you know how selfish you sound right now? You know what my mum and sisters were going through. Dad's leaving shook them hard. I had to be there for them.'

'I didn't begrudge that.'

'It sounds like you did.'

'Of course I didn't!' she protested vehemently.

'But I didn't hear from you for days or weeks at a time.'

'I was busy with work.'

It was the one area of his life where he'd known what he was doing. Where he knew the actions he needed to take and the direction he wanted to go. At a time when everything else around him was precarious, work was the one area he was in control.

'I know,' she said. 'But it made me realise how your life was so separate from mine. We were at different stages. You were building an empire; I didn't have any clue what I'd do after I graduated.'

'I don't understand why you didn't talk to me about it instead of ignoring me,' he said.

'You were never there for me to talk to!'

He shook his head. He'd always tried to spend time with her when he could. He'd been juggling many priorities at the time. He tried to be the rock his family needed and at the same time develop his business from the ground up. He hadn't wanted to put his worries onto her shoulders.

He grimaced. But there was some truth to her accusation.

Saira already had too much on her plate at that time. She'd been busy with her second-year exams. And offering comfort to Miranda, who wasn't coping well with their parents' situation. He hadn't wanted Saira to have to be his solace too. Besides, she was going to the States for a year. With the situation at home he couldn't move abroad—and he hadn't wanted to rely on Saira when she wouldn't always be there.

So each time he'd wanted to go to her, to spend time simply being with her, he'd thrown himself into his work instead. But he'd always thought he'd been there if she asked him.

Now he was hearing it wasn't enough.

The frustration and loneliness of that time threatened to overwhelm him. He couldn't tell her that, so he turned to irritation as a defence. 'What were you expecting? Me to dance attendance on you every moment? You know, your family may treat you like a princess, but that doesn't make you one.'

'Don't bring my family into it!' She sat up even straighter.

'I don't have to; they were always there. We had to date in secret when you were at school, because your parents didn't want you to have a boyfriend until you were eighteen. Then we couldn't tell anyone about us when you were at university because you were worried your parents wouldn't like you dating a non-Indian.'

Saira made a sound, as if choking down her aggravation. 'Much as I love listening to your revisionist history, my family were not a factor once I went to university. I was ready to tell them and then—' She broke off.

'And then what?'

Her shoulders sagged. 'And then you said love was for idiots and you were never getting married. I couldn't see the point of telling my family about a fling we were having.'

He pressed his lips together. He *had* said that—straight after spending days with his mother crying on his shoulder.

'It wasn't a fling.'

'Well, it wasn't going to be anything long term, was it?' she challenged him.

'It wasn't going to be marriage, no,' he admitted. 'I don't make any secret of that. I don't see any point in getting married. But I didn't put an end date on our relationship.'

He was too much like his father ever to risk marriage. Unless children were involved. In those circumstances he would do his duty and give them the security they deserved. But it was a moot point—he never intended to have children.

'But, you see, I didn't know that,' she said. 'When we broke up the first time we agreed we were too young. But we always spoke about being together in the future. Maybe I was immature, but in my mind that meant marriage.'

'I never made you any promises.' He'd learnt from his father that promises weren't kept.

'No, but you broke my heart anyway!' she cried out.

His body stilled, ice water running through him as she accused him of doing the one thing he swore he would never do. He refused to believe it. He was not his father.

'You broke mine too,' he said simply.

'No,' she said vehemently, shaking her head. 'No. Don't you dare say that! You cared about me, but you never loved me. Love is for idiots, remember? Your ego may have been bruised, but your heart wasn't affected.'

He puffed out a long breath, not wanting to listen to her words. She was acting as if she was the only one who'd been affected by their break-up. At the time he hadn't been one of the Six-Month Men. He was telling the truth—he hadn't put an end date to their relationship. He hadn't offered marriage, but she'd been the closest he'd ever come to long term. Until she went away and forgot about him.

'What about you? Your heartbreak didn't last long, did it?' He spat out the resentment he'd been harbouring for so many years. 'You left, and the next thing I knew Miranda told me you were getting married.' It had been a gut-punch when he heard that news.

'Come on,' she scoffed. 'That was three years later! Oh, this is a waste of time; we're going round in circles.'

She got out of bed, picked up her clothes and went into the en suite bathroom.

Nathan lay back against the pillow, covering his eyes with his arm. That had gone as well as he'd expected. He'd been right to want to avoid discussions of the past. Nothing positive ever came of it.

People always viewed the past through their own lens. She thought their relationship had been over because he hadn't been there for her. He thought she'd run away.

He glanced at the bathroom door. She was getting ready to run away again.

He debated trying to dissuade her.

There was no point. He should never have let it get this far in the first place. He'd let their strong sexual connection override his good sense. He'd meant to keep their relationship as light as all his other ones, but instead he'd constantly broken his rules and found reasons to continue it.

He frowned.

Why had he kept their relationship going? Why was he unable to walk away from Saira?

He gave himself a shake. It didn't matter. He didn't want to explore the reasons and they didn't matter anyway.

Saira might have been lashing out at him, but she'd been telling the truth. He'd broken her heart when he'd told her he didn't believe in love or marriage. She'd cared about him and he'd hurt her to the core. But nothing had changed. He still had nothing to offer her. If he didn't end things now, he would only hurt her again in the long run. If they broke up now they would be able to walk away with their hearts intact.

Saira let the water sluice over her, trying to wake herself. Her sleep had been fitful. Perhaps that was the reason she was feeling slightly nauseous.

This whole thing was a mess. They'd agreed to draw a line under the past. She'd always expected the discussion of what had happened would be the beginning of the end for their affair, but here she was, bringing it up anyway.

What was she even doing?

It wasn't as if she was looking for a long-term relationship. But it was hard being with Nathan when memories kept surfacing. They'd got on so well when they were younger. He had always been one of the most interesting people she knew. Even when they hadn't been dating she'd enjoyed spending time with him. His personality meshed with hers in a unique way. She didn't want to lose that connection with him again.

Not being in contact with him after their relationship ended had been one of the big losses of her life—not the same as losing her husband, of course, but emotionally difficult nonetheless. Now she understood why Nathan hadn't come after her—he blamed her.

She still remembered the maelstrom of feelings she'd had for Nathan when they were younger. Deep and all-encompassing. It had been difficult for her to move on from him. Move on to the safety and comfort of Dilip.

She loved Dilip, but they'd had an arranged marriage, with their love developing after they married. It had been soft and gentle, and losing him so suddenly hurt unbearably. It had taken her a long time before her grief subsided enough for her to be ready to move forward with her life.

She never wanted to feel anything as devastating as that again. And that was the risk if she carried on an affair with Nathan. She could admit that.

Physical attraction she could deal with. Ignore it if necessary. Far more dangerous was liking him again. With Nathan, liking led all too easily to love—a path she couldn't go down. Wouldn't. It almost broke her the first time.

She hadn't thought through the repercussions of their relationship when they were on holiday. Not thinking things through properly when it came to Nathan was apparently one of her major flaws.

Now she had no choice. It was far better to end their sexual relationship now, when her feelings were still nascent and could be suppressed. Then they could work on being friends, which was vital with Miranda's wedding come up.

She'd allowed herself one more night. Time was up.

Nathan was making coffee when she finally walked into the living area.

'Are you hungry?' he asked, giving her a quick glance. 'I've made some breakfast.'

His expression was completely blank—as if they hadn't argued minutes before. If she needed any reminder he didn't really care about her, he was making it very clear.

'Thanks,' she said, sitting down to a plate of waffles with berries, drizzled with maple syrup. She glanced at the mixing bowl on the dryer and the waffle maker on the counter.

They ate in silence. Occasionally she would glance his way and notice him watching her. Usually he would smile or wink whenever their eyes met, but this morning his face remained sombre.

'You're right,' she admitted, putting her cutlery down and hugging her coffee mug with both hands. 'It was me who ran away.'

He paused, then expelled a breath. 'No, you're right too. I did start to pull away from you.'

She snorted. 'Please don't start arguing with me about who's to blame again.'

'It's not about blame, though, is it, Saira? Although I have blamed you for the way it ended in the past, I should have realised you were thinking about marriage. We never defined our relationship.'

'No, we didn't.' She gave a wry smile. 'I assumed it was what I wanted it to be. I was so young, and immature for my age. I couldn't believe we could be in a relationship and having sex if we weren't going to stay together,'

'I didn't mean to lead you on. I am sorry about that,' he replied.

He was bending his head, as if hiding his guilt. But there was no emotion in his tone—he could have been reciting from a dictionary.

'I didn't think we had a future. My parents' twenty-five-year marriage got thrown in the dustbin—what chance did we have?'

She frowned. Why did he keep comparing himself to his father? Couldn't he tell he was nothing like him? But his future relationships no longer mattered to her, so instead of challenging his assertion, she nodded. 'What I don't get is why you were so aloof when I came back.'

'We didn't end it cleanly. You went silent, stopped contacting me. I had to rely on Miranda to hear any news about you. That wasn't right, Saira. After what we had, that wasn't right.'

She hung her head at the deserved condemnation in his tone. 'I'm sorry.'

She was silent for a few moments, her mind processing their conversation. Nathan had used the past tense to describe his thoughts on their future, but nothing had changed for him. He still didn't believe in love or marriage. Was still certain he couldn't make a long-term commitment.

She wished she could be the woman who showed him how wrong he was—that he cared deeply and had the capacity to have a long and happy marriage. But that wasn't her role. Too much had gone on in the past for her to be the one to convince him. He wouldn't believe her.

And too much had happened to make her believe in a happily-ever-after with him. She cared about him intensely, probably still loved him, but until he was ready to admit he could love and was ready to accept her love, nothing would change.

She couldn't carry on in a relationship where her feelings would grow stronger with every day knowing that he would never admit he even *had* feelings. It would be too painful.

She straightened her shoulders with determination. At the end of the day, this relationship was going nowhere. She was an independent, capable woman. She was in control of her future. She could live happily on her own. As she'd always intended when she returned to England. Her attraction to Nathan had derailed her for a while, but she could ignore the hormonal urges the same way she could ignore the stirrings of her foolish heart. It was safer that way. She wouldn't get hurt.

She took a deep breath. 'We both love Miranda, and she's going to need us while she plans her wedding.'

'Yes.'

'We agreed to make an effort for her, and then things got confused because we brought sex into the mix.' She raised her hand to prevent him from interrupting. 'If we keep on as we are, we will inevitably end up fighting. I would rather end it now, while we can be comfortable in each other's company. I don't want to risk us ending a few weeks down the road because we have a big argument, or because you get bored with me. That would be awkward.'

Nathan straightened, his face a mask. 'If that's what you want.'

She nodded.

It was that easy? No arguments? No attempt to convince her to change her mind?

It was over just like that.

It was strangely anti-climactic.

What had she expected? A protestation of love?

She hopped off her stool, reaching for the counter as a wave of dizziness overcame her.

Nathan was immediately by her side. 'Are you okay?'

'Yes, I'm fine. Just a bit dizzy again.'

'Are you sure?'

'Yes.' She ignored the clear concern on his face and steeled herself. 'What? Did you think I was swooning because our break-up is too much for me to take?'

He pursed his lips together. 'This is the second time you've almost fainted. Perhaps you should see a doctor.'

'Maybe you're right. I can get anaemic when I'm due my period. I'm sure that's all it is.'

He nodded, but didn't say anything, so she grabbed her things and gave him a kiss on the cheek.

This was the right decision for her. She was walking away from him again. But this time it was on her own terms. It was already hurting so much, but it was inevitable that sooner or later they would end things and say goodbye. There would always be a goodbye ahead.

The dizziness and nausea hit her again as soon as she was on the tube. Was this a physical manifestation of the utter loss she was feeling inside? What was wrong with her?

CHAPTER EIGHT

ALL THE DIFFERENT instruction leaflets scattered on her counter said the same thing—the best time to take a test was first thing in the morning. Saira knew this already. She didn't need to read the instructions to know what to do. But reading them was a good distraction from thinking about why she needed the tests...

She ran her fingers through her hair. She could be worrying about nothing. Probably was. This was a situation she was all too familiar with, and each time she was left disappointed.

Saira picked up one of the boxes. How many times had she bought one of these, full of excitement, full of joy, and then seen Dilip's crestfallen face each time she told him the negative news?

Apart from that one time. Which she didn't let herself think about. Couldn't let herself think about.

She took a couple of deep, centring breaths and focused on the boxes in front of her. After all those times when she'd yearned for a positive result, she couldn't be pregnant from a fling. Could she?

She hadn't even considered it a possibility until that morning. When Dilip died, Saira had put away her ovulation kits and thermometers and trackers, never expecting to need them again.

It was only when she saw her stock of unused sanitary supplies and put them together with her dizzy episodes and mild morning nausea that she even entertained the thought.

The hope?

The previous times she'd taken these tests she'd been part of a loving, committed couple, for whom a child would have been a much-wanted addition to their family.

This time it couldn't be more different.

She'd returned to England to start again. Get a job. Find her own place. Be independent. Her future plans hadn't included having a child.

But those plans were based on her false assumption she would need to be in a relationship before a child could be part of the picture. Life didn't care about her assumptions. If she were pregnant she could easily adjust those plans, and would happily do so.

Pregnant.

Could it be possible?

She half-laughed, half-cried at the prospect. The fear, the worry, the doubts had already started to creep in. She held her hands over her stomach. Even a positive pregnancy test wasn't a guarantee of happiness. Those memories were getting harder to hold back. Threatening to overwhelm her.

She needed to be practical. She deliberately turned her thoughts to Nathan. To how he would react. It was bad enough trying to keep her thoughts in order, without adding the extra complication of how to involve him, the father of her possible child. She had no idea how to handle this situation. Was there some etiquette for telling someone you'd had a fling with that you might be pregnant with their baby?

How would he take the news? Not well, that was for sure. He didn't do long term. He didn't want commitment. A child was a life-long commitment. You couldn't get more long term than that. This was probably the last thing he wanted.

Her phone rang.

'Hey, Saira,' Miranda said. 'Are you in this afternoon?'

'Yes. Do you want to come over?'

'No—I meant to call you earlier, but I forgot, sorry.'

Saira's brow furrowed 'Okay. What's up?'

'Nathan was here for lunch. He offered to drop round my wedding binder and some magazines for you to look at. I told him I could post them, but he said it's on his way. He left over an hour ago, so he should be there soon.'

Ice pulsed through her body. Nathan was on his way. She hadn't seen him since she'd ended their fling three weeks ago. She wasn't prepared to see him. Not now. Not with this pile of boxes in front of her.

'Are you okay?' Miranda asked.

'Yes, of course—I'm fine. Why wouldn't I be?'

'You didn't say anything for a few minutes. Isn't this the first time you'll see him since you broke up?'

Saira resisted the urge to insist they hadn't broken up because they had never been a real couple.

'Why would that bother me? It was never a big deal between me and Nathan.'

Hopefully, she sounded believable. She changed the conversation to Operation Wedding, chatting for a few more minutes before Miranda rang off.

She leant on her elbows, pulled her cheeks down, then rubbed her face. She'd thought she'd have more time before involving Nathan. Take the test, at least. But he was on his way. Should she tell him when he came?

Perhaps she should wait to tell him until she'd entered her second trimester. She knew better than anyone how fragile new life was in the first few weeks. But what if he wanted to be at the first scan? Didn't she owe him the chance to be involved from the outset? If he even wanted to be involved…

She muffled a scream. There were too many unknowns. Instead of speculating on possibilities, she needed to concentrate on the steps she *could* control.

The doorbell rang, causing Saira to knock all the boxes off the counter. She hurriedly gathered them up, then shoved them into a drawer. Taking a couple of deep breaths, she went to answer the door.

Slightly surprised when Nathan accepted her invitation to come in rather than leaving straight after dropping off the binder and magazines, her eyes kept straying to him while she made them some tea.

His thick dark hair looked slightly longer than usual, beginning to wave in the front. Her fingers flexed with the muscle memory of running through those strands. The inky blue of his simple but expensive cashmere jumper stretched across his broad shoulders, the perfect foil to his piercing eyes. It wasn't fair. He was cover-model-gorgeous while she was the personification of Death.

At least pregnancy would explain her roller-coaster of emotions since they'd ended things. Life was a funny thing. Years ago she'd dreamt of raising a family with Nathan. Look where they were now.

She made a rueful sound.

'Are you okay?' Nathan asked.

She needed to pull herself together. Start acting naturally. 'Yes, I'm fine. Thanks.' She brought the drinks over.

'Are you sure you're okay? You don't look well,' he said.

'Well, that's flattering. Thank you.' She made a face at him.

'You know you're always beautiful. You seem a little tired, though.'

'I am a little tired,' she agreed, hoping to keep the conversation light. 'It's been a hectic couple of weeks.'

He frowned. 'Did you see the doctor about your dizzy spells?'

'No.' She waved her hand, dismissing the need. She didn't need a doctor's appointment to determine whether she was pregnant.

'How's work?' she asked. Discussions about her health were heading towards dangerous territory.

'Good—busy.'

'I read in the papers you completed that acquisition.'

'Yes, it went through a week ago.'

He was so cold and abrupt. This was worse than when they'd seen each other at Miranda's engagement party. The familiar prickling sensation at the back of her eyes energised her to stand up, excusing herself to go to the bathroom.

She sluiced water over her face. This was ridiculous. She needed to pull herself together. Concentrate on the facts. She didn't know for certain if she was pregnant. If there was a baby, Nathan was the father. She didn't know how he would react, but it was information he deserved to have.

In an ideal world she would wait until she'd taken the test before she told him, but after today she didn't know when she would see him again if it wasn't something to do with Miranda's wedding. That would not be an appropriate time to tell him the news. Wouldn't it be better to tell him in person rather than over the phone?

Did it matter how he reacted? She had always longed to have a child. She had more than enough love to raise one on her own. She was more than capable. If Nathan wanted to be involved that was a benefit, not a requirement. She could love the baby for both of them.

She straightened her shoulders, inhaled deeply, then walked back to the lounge.

'Are you sure you're all right, Saira? You weren't being sick, were you?'

Saira smiled wanly. 'I'm okay, Nathan.'

This would be a great time to segue into telling him the truth…

His brows furrowed. 'I think you should make a doctor's appointment to be on the safe side.'

'I don't need to. I—'

'I know you don't like being told what to do, but—'

'I think I'm pregnant,' she blurted out.

Nathan blinked then shook his head.

Pregnant.

Had he heard correctly? Had she said *pregnant*? Thank goodness he was already sitting down.

Pregnant.

She wasn't ill, though, which was a relief.

He'd known there was something different from her appearance. She looked beautiful, as always, but now there was a haunting quality to her beauty, a fragility he hadn't seen before. Her cheekbones were more pronounced. Had she lost weight?

He reached out to rub his thumb along her face but managed to pull his hand back before making contact.

He hadn't expected her to say she was pregnant. No, she'd said she 'thought' she was pregnant. What did she mean…*thought*?

He stood up and started to walk—from the lounge door to the window, several times, barely noticing the view of Russell Square—as he tried to process the information.

Saira was pregnant. Or she thought she could be pregnant. With his baby? Of course with his baby. If she were pregnant he would be the father.

His steps faltered. He could be a father. He never wanted to be a father. He didn't know how to be a father. What if he disappointed his child the way his father always let him down?

Saira's voice broke into his thoughts. 'Please stop pacing.'

He paused, then turned to face her. She was huddled in an armchair, her hands hugging her mug to her heart.

He nodded his head as he continued to process his thoughts while he stood still.

'Can you sit down? I don't want you looming over me.'

She looked defeated. He took a step towards her, then stopped. He needed to keep his distance until he could clear his head.

He sat down again. 'It's a lot to take in.'

'For me, too.'

He nodded. It was a lot for both of them to wrap their heads around. He needed to take control, so they could start making decisions and plans. The first step was to find out for certain.

'You said you *think* you're pregnant?'

'I haven't taken a test yet, but there have been a few signs.'

He nodded again. Keeping it formal—clinical,

even—was the best course of action. 'What about your period? Have you missed it?'

'I don't know. They haven't been regular since—' She broke off, putting her mug down,then wrapping her arms round her stomach in a gesture of self-protection.

'I can buy a pregnancy test.'

'I have loads. I was planning to take one today.'

He narrowed his eyes. How long had she suspected she was pregnant? There was no way Saira would have kept her pregnancy a secret from him, but even though she already bought a test she hadn't contacted him.

'When were you planning to tell me?'

'I don't know,' she told him simply. 'It's new to me too. I only suspected I could be pregnant this morning. I don't know if I am, and I know the stats about pregnancies in the first trimester.'

Her face was a mask and her body closed in, as if she was protecting herself.

'Perhaps you should take the test while I'm here, so we know for sure.' Once he knew, he could start making plans for their future.

'It's best to take the test in the morning.'

He stared at her, unblinking. Did he sense some reluctance to get confirmation one way or another? 'You can take one now and another in the morning.'

She sighed, but made no effort to move.

'Saira?' He couldn't understand her reluctance. Wasn't it better if they knew the situation?

'Fine,' Saira said in a frustrated tone. 'I'll take the test now.'

'Good. Do you want me to come with you?' he offered, in case she was feeling nervous. He raised his eyebrows, questioning the curious expression she was giving him.

'Nate, I'm about to wee on a stick. I certainly do not want you there.'

His lips twitched. Trust Saira to bring some humour into the situation.

He resumed his pacing once she'd disappeared into the bathroom. Soon they would have their answer. What did he hope it would be?

He'd never imagined being a father. This wasn't something in his life's plan. He would have to make many adjustments and accommodations to be actively involved with his child. He wasn't going to be like his father—a phantom presence, floating in and out at his own convenience. If the test was positive, Nathan's life was going to change dramatically.

Was it usual for prospective fathers to feel this sense of overwhelm? And fear. Fear he was too much like his own father to know how to be one for his child. Fear he wouldn't be in his child's life as much as he wanted.

Saira came out the bathroom waving her phone. 'I've set the timer. Now we wait.'

She sat back in the armchair, her hands steepled together, resting against her mouth. He resisted the urge to wrap her in his arms, comfort her. She had been around when his father had waltzed in and out. She would rightly worry he was going to disappear the same way. He wanted to say something to reassure her that if she was pregnant he would be by her side.

They both started when the timer went off. They walked to the bathroom and waited for the words to appear in the small test window.

Pregnant 3+ weeks

There it was. The truth. She was pregnant. He was going to be a father.

He swallowed the lump in his throat.

How could he be a father? He didn't know the first thing about being one. His father had been the worst role model, and he never wanted to put children through what he and his sisters had gone through.

That was moot now. He was going to be a father.

Saira burst into tears, covering her face in her hands. This time without hesitation he gathered her into his arms and carried her into the lounge, settling on the sofa with her on his lap. Of course this would be overwhelming for her.

'It's fine, darling. Everything's fine.' He stroked her hair, frowning when she cried harder.

'You don't know that.' She sobbed into his chest. In a small voice she said, 'I'm so worried. Things don't work out just because you want them to.'

He closed his eyes, fearing she would mention termination. 'What do you mean?'

'I've been here before. Positive pregnancy test. We were so happy.'

It shouldn't have shocked him to learn she had been pregnant by her husband. He didn't resent her past relationship with Dilip—but at the same time he didn't want to know all the details about her marriage. Only now her past experience was causing her to worry.

He couldn't change what had happened with her previous pregnancy. Nor could he promise everything would be fine with this one. The only thing he could do was reassure her that he would be there for her. And take as much stress off her plate as he could.

'We should probably discuss what we're going to do,' he said.

'I hope to have this baby. I think that's worth saying,' she said forcefully.

'Obviously that's your decision alone, but for the record I would never suggest you shouldn't.'

'I know, but I felt you should know upfront what I plan. There's not a decision to make here.

It's made.' She paused, and then added as an afterthought, 'As far as it's in my control.'

His eyes widened as deep pain flashed in her eyes. Something bad must have happened with her previous pregnancy, but asking questions at this time wouldn't ease her worries. Instead, he would concentrate on practicalities.

'In that case we should discuss what we plan to do in the future.'

'Not now—not until I'm through my first trimester.'

He nodded, not really understanding why that mattered. 'When will that be?'

Her expression was blank. 'I don't know.' She laughed without real humour. 'I don't know when I got pregnant. We used protection! It could have been any occasion—' Her voice was rising as she broke off. 'I'll arrange an appointment with a doctor and a dating scan.'

A scan. A chance to see his child. Would that make it more real?

'Will you let me know what you've arranged? I'd like to go with you.'

She nodded.

They sat in silence for a few moments, both seemingly unable to contemplate this huge, unexpected change in their future plans.

'I'm still quite tired,' Saira said after a while. 'If you don't mind, I'm going to have a nap. I'll contact you once I've got some dates.'

The urge to stay behind and take care of her warred with his instinctive sense that she wouldn't appreciate it. He wouldn't do anything to agitate her. Not now. Not when she was carrying his child.

'Good. You look after yourself…' All words were inadequate. 'Call me if you need anything. Any time.' He bent to drop a kiss on her forehead.

Once outside her apartment he expelled a breath. That was the last thing he'd expected to find out when he'd offered to take his sister's wedding binder to Saira. He hadn't thought much beyond seeing her again.

He was going to be a dad.

He might never have chosen this for himself. But now the decision had been taken from him he would be the best father he could and do right by Saira and his child. He wouldn't abandon them the way his father abandoned his family.

This might not be what he would have chosen for his life, but he would do his duty. He would make a commitment and stick with it. He would be there for his child. He would be there for Saira.

CHAPTER NINE

SAIRA BREATHED IN for a count of seven and out for a count of eleven, using the anxiety techniques she'd learnt after Dilip died while she waited for her name to be called.

This wasn't the first time she'd sat in a hospital waiting for an ultrasound, but she'd never made it to the first dating scan before. She'd purposefully kept her mind off what happened with her first pregnancy. The sorrow was always there, just beneath the surface, but she coped by grieving fully for what she'd lost and trying to look forward with hope.

She pressed a hand against her still-flat stomach. 'Please be okay, baby,' she whispered.

Nathan placed a reassuring hand on her knee. She gave him a grateful smile. His confidence and arrogant disbelief that anything bad could happen gave her the hope she was afraid to believe in herself. Earlier that morning he'd sat patiently in the waiting room while she'd had her booking appointment and his patience paid off when they were able to schedule a dating scan the same day. One of the benefits of the care offered at the most renowned private maternity hospital in London.

When Nathan first told her he'd arranged the booking appointment for her here, she'd been fuming. It was just like him to try to take charge. It was great that he was taking such an interest in the pregnancy, but he needed to recognise *she* was the one who was pregnant. *She* was the primary decision-maker.

Of course she would discuss things with him. They probably wouldn't agree on everything, so it was more important than ever she stood her ground from the outset.

The pale lilac tones of the waiting room, the pristine furniture and the top-quality equipment visible from her seat calmed her slightly, certain her baby would receive excellent care. She was prepared to give Nathan the benefit of the doubt on this call. If there was one thing they would agree on it was to have the best quality of care for their baby. And not having to wait for the appointment was a bonus.

She looked at him out of the corner of her eye. He was reading some of the pamphlets from the waiting area about tests available. She knew this situation wasn't what he wanted. He was being forced into fatherhood. Because of that he was doing what he always did—throwing himself into it, making the best outcome he could. She'd watched him to do it for his mother and sisters after his father left. She didn't want him to feel she was a responsibility. She could take care of herself.

Finally, they were called in for the scan. Because she was unsure of her due date the radiographer suggested they try an abdominal scan in the first instance. After watching her press a few buttons and make some facial expressions Saira couldn't interpret, memories of the last time she'd been in this position came flooding back. The concerned, sad look on the technician's face, her hasty exit from the room and her return with a senior doctor…

Trying to suppress the images, she turned to look up at the ceiling, using her breathing technique again.

'Would you like to see your baby for the first time?'

The radiographer turned the monitor towards them. Saira stared at the image on the screen, her eyes filling with tears. She glanced in Nathan's direction. He was staring intently at the screen. Was that moisture in his eyes too? She laced her fingers through his. He turned to her with a smile, bringing her hand to his lips to press a quick kiss to it.

She tried to concentrate as the radiographer gave them more details, but all she could see was the pulsing image in front of her. Her baby's heartbeat. This was their baby. She had given up hope this would ever happen.

'From the measurements here, and the details you provided, you're around thirteen weeks. I've finished here,' the radiographer continued, after making a few more notations. 'If you go back to the waiting room someone will come to fetch you when the consultant is ready to see you.'

'Consultant?' Nathan queried. 'Is there something wrong?'

'My notes show Ms Dey has been referred to a consultant. You can ask for details at Reception. I'll print some photos for you to take. At later scans we can arrange a video too.'

During their brief wait for the consultant, Saira was handed the scan photos. Holding them, she couldn't focus on anything else.

Everything looked fine.

She was going to have a baby.

Once they were in the consultant's office she was vaguely aware of Nathan speaking, saying something about due dates, conception and consultants—but she couldn't tear her attention away from the photos.

The consultant looked through the notes on her monitor. 'You've been referred to me because of your previous molar pregnancy,' she said.

'I see.'

Saira glanced at Nathan. He frowned at her before he turned back to the doctor.

'That was three years ago?' the consultant asked.

'Yes, around then.'

'And you went to all your follow-up appointments?'

'Yes.'

'For the requisite six months?'

Saira nodded.

'And there have been no other pregnancies before or since?' the doctor continued.

'No.'

The consultant typed a few notes. 'Right, then, Ms Dey. This pregnancy looks good. The baby is growing well. No signs of any problems with your uterus. I would prefer, as a precaution, to keep you under consultant supervision, but it's your choice if you want to go for midwife-led.'

'We'll go for consultant care,' Nathan said.

'Maybe we should discuss this?' Saira countered. She had to nip his control tendencies in the bud.

'No, there's no cost issue here,' he replied.

She pressed her lips together but didn't say anything. This wasn't a conversation they needed to have in public, but Nathan was going to find out being the father of her baby didn't mean he could ignore or overrule her views.

* * *

On the drive back she constantly stared at the scan pictures, reassuring herself that this wasn't a dream. She was really pregnant—and in her second trimester.

Getting past the first trimester was a major milestone—one she'd come so close to before. She scrunched her eyes tightly, still terrified at the prospect of something going wrong. She was already opening herself to more loss and hurt because she already loved her baby with all her heart—but there was nothing she could do to stop that. Loving her child was as natural and inevitable as breathing.

She glanced quickly at Nathan. He had been silent the entire journey. What was he thinking? He'd been clear from the start he didn't believe in long-term commitments. Parenthood was as long term as you could get.

Once upon a time it would have been her dream come true to be having a baby with Nathan as the father. But so much water had passed under the bridge since then. After their tense argument the day she'd broken things off, there was too much hurt and history for them ever to find common ground. All it seemed to prove was that they couldn't make it as a couple, no matter how much she wanted to.

She'd never understood why he believed he couldn't do commitment; it was unusual for a man who was brimming over with self-confidence to be convinced he could fail at something.

She grimaced. His father's actions had a much deeper and lasting negative impact than perhaps he realised. Couldn't Nathan see what a great capacity for caring and love he had? She only needed to recall the countless ways he took care of his mother and sisters to know that. There was no doubt in her mind he would be an amazing dad.

She expelled a breath. They couldn't avoid a proper talk about the future. They had to find a way that worked for both of them. One where she kept her independence.

What chance was there for them to forge an understanding around how they would raise their child if their past issues remained unresolved? Did Nathan even recognise they needed to address it if they had any hope of coming to an arrangement?

'Are you okay?' she asked when he pulled up outside her apartment. 'I know it's a lot to take in. I can hardly believe it myself.'

'We need to talk,' he said.

She nodded. They had a lot to discuss, but she needed to get her own mind around the situation, think about what *she* wanted first.

'I know,' she replied. 'But can we do it another day? I'm tired, and I think we both need to process a bit more before we talk through things properly.'

Without waiting for his reply, she exited the car and went into her building.

Nathan stood next to the window of Saira's living room. watching the activity on the street as he tried to marshal his thoughts. Had it only been five days since they'd seen their baby on the ultrasound?

In a little over six months he was going to be a father…a dad. He might never have planned to have children, but pregnancy was always a possibility when you had sex. He knew a child was the only reason he would ever contemplate marriage.

Maybe he didn't know how to be a good father yet, but he had a great example for how *not* to be one. He would never make the same mistakes his father had. The only thing his father had done right was marry his mother when she'd found out she was pregnant with him. The least he could do for Saira was offer her the same. He would do his duty. But, unlike his father, he had no intention of leaving when he got bored. He didn't make commitments lightly—when he did, he stuck with them.

He turned as Saira walked in with mugs of tea. He grimaced, annoyed with himself—he should have thought through this moment better, brought a ring with him. But it was too late to do anything about that now. Saira would probably enjoy picking out a ring for herself. And it wasn't as if this was a romantic proposal. Was a ring even necessary?

'I think we should get married around Christmas,' he said, sitting down next to her.

A winter wedding would be the perfect way to start their future together. As soon-to-be parents, he reminded himself. This was about the baby, not him and Saira as a couple. Christmas was a time for families. He always tried to spend it with his mother and sisters. And the following Christmas he would have his own family to spend the time with. He smiled inwardly as he imagined Saira and his child in front of a large, brightly decorated tree.

He glanced at Saira when he realised she hadn't responded.

She was looking at him blankly, then she made a choking sound. 'Sorry, what?' she asked, shaking her head and smiling.

His eyes narrowed. He had been quite clear. He sighed and with great patience said, 'It would be good if we were married around Christmas. I was planning to spend a few days with my mother and sisters over the holidays, so my family will be around. I can send my plane for your parents.'

Saira covered her mouth with her fingers for

a moment, as if she were holding back a laugh. Humour wasn't the reaction he was expecting.

'I'm sorry. Are you being serious?' she asked.

'Of course. I'm asking you to marry me.'

'Well, you're not actually *asking*,' she muttered.

He frowned. Had she been expecting him to go down on one knee? 'Getting married is the right thing to do,' he insisted.

At that she did burst out laughing. 'Right thing?' she exclaimed. She placed a hand on her chest, widening her eyes and fluttering her eyelashes. 'That's truly so romantic.'

He pursed his lips. He could do without her mockery when they had serious matters to discuss. 'We need to be practical right now.'

'Yes. By all means let's be practical.' She sighed. 'But getting married isn't about practicality. Or at least it shouldn't be.'

He closed his eyes, gathering his patience. He should have anticipated she would be difficult about this. She was going to fight him all the way if he didn't get a handle on the situation. Perhaps she didn't believe he was prepared to offer her commitment—offer their child the security it deserved. He had to find the right argument, the right words to persuade her.

'It will be best for our child if we're married,' he said.

'Says who?'

He definitely should have come better prepared. 'I'm sure there are studies. I can get my assistant to send you some research.'

Saira rolled her eyes. 'This would be so funny if you weren't being serious right now. I don't care what *research* says. I'm not marrying you.'

'Would you care to tell me why?'

'I don't plan on getting married again.'

'Did you plan on having a child?' he challenged.

'Maybe not.'

'Plans change and we need to adapt. I'm prepared to adapt. I'm offering to do the right thing and marry you.' He rubbed the back of his neck. 'I don't understand why you're being difficult.'

'Difficult?' Her voice's pitch went an octave higher. 'Disagreeing with you doesn't make me "difficult".'

'I'm not going to abandon my child.'

He would be part of his child's life. He was offering them security, protection—he could meet their every need. What more did she want?

'I don't think you would. Marriage isn't the solution, though. It would be different if we were in love, or even in a relationship.'

He raised an eyebrow. He was offering marriage. He wasn't offering love. He couldn't. She knew that. He'd never made a secret about that.

'You never even wanted a long-term commitment,' she continued. 'And I'm not going to trap you into one.'

'I want to get married,' he protested, although he couldn't deny the accuracy of her statement. He'd never thought he would have children or get married. But that didn't matter any more. They had a baby on the way. He could and would be there for his child. Now he'd made the conscious decision to be part of his baby's life he wasn't going anywhere—he would never rip his child's heart apart the way his father had done. And Saira would finally be a part of his life as well. They would be together the way he'd always…

He refused to let his thoughts continue down that path. 'It's not a trap if I'm asking you.'

'It really is. People don't have to get married because they're having a baby. My dad's not going to be there holding a shotgun.' She paused for a few moments. 'Be sensible, Nathan. You can't marry every woman you get pregnant.'

His mouth slackened. He closed his eyes briefly, pinching the bridge of his nose. 'I haven't got any other woman pregnant.'

'That you know of.'

'I know,' he insisted.

How could she even suggest he wouldn't know about it?

He inhaled slowly, rubbing his hand over his face. 'None of my exes are pregnant or have had my secret baby. And I'm not going to argue with you about an unrealistic hypothetical situation.'

'Okay, but you don't marry someone because they're pregnant. At least, I don't think you should. I know you think you're doing the honourable thing here, but it isn't necessary. There has to be more to marriage. Believe me, I know. How can you even think about spending your life with someone when they can't even hold your interest for six months? The rest of your life! How is that rational?'

He was silent. He would have done his duty whatever the circumstances. Wouldn't he? Marriage was always the correct step. There was no point speculating on whether he would have done his duty if someone else had been pregnant. Saira was the one who was pregnant. And he couldn't imagine anyone else being the mother of his child. Everything else was irrelevant.

'It makes sense for us to be married. You know it's the right thing.'

She shook her head. 'Stop saying that. It's not the right thing for me,' she said with a shrug. 'I don't believe it would be the right thing for our child in our circumstances. You more than anyone should know that.'

'What does that mean?'

'You told me your dad stayed with your mum for the children. It made your dad miserable.'

His narrowed his eyes. It always came back

to his father—to comparisons with him. 'My father was a selfish man who abandoned his family. He cheated on my mother constantly. Did I ever tell you that?'

'Your parents should never have married. They were miserable. I'm not going to put you through the same thing.'

'I would never cheat on you.'

'I know. Instead, you would be stuck with me for the rest of your life, like some kind of punishment. You would resent me and be unhappy.'

He shook his head. He could make it work. If he put his mind to it, he could be a good husband and father. It wouldn't be a punishment being in his son or daughter's life. He would be happy being married to Saira.

'What's more, *I* would be unhappy,' Saira continued.

His shoulders slumped. He would never want that. 'I want to be involved with my child,' he said. 'I want to be a good father. I want to be there for her or him. The best way for me to do that is if I'm married to you. I don't promise to love you. I'm not capable of that emotion. We have a strong basis for marriage without bringing emotions into it. You should consider my proposition seriously.'

'I've already told you it's not happening. We barely know each other anymore! And I'm not going to force you into a marriage you don't want.'

Nathan sighed. 'I wouldn't be asking if I didn't want this.'

She shook her head.

What could he say that would convince her marriage was not only the best thing for their child, it was the best thing for him too? Without marriage, Saira could run away again—leave him, taking his child with her. He would never let that happen.

'Can't we take marriage off the table for now?' she pleaded. 'We'll never get anywhere if our discussions stall arguing about something that's never going to happen. There must be lots of options other than marriage. Of course you'll have all your parental rights, and I'm sure we can work out generous visitation.'

That wasn't enough. He didn't want to be a part-time father. He wanted a proper family.

'Think about what I'm offering, Saira. I can give you and our child a great life. You don't even have a job. I can give you financial security. Neither of you will want for anything.'

'Money isn't everything,' she said, in a neutral tone that caused a knot in his stomach.

'Money has its advantages.'

'You're right. It does. Maybe I'm not a billionaire, but I have more than enough money to take care of my child and raise them comfortably even without a job.'

'Really?' He raised his eyebrows. 'How do you propose to do that?'

'The thing is, Nathan, money has always been a tool for you to get your own way. But this time it's not going to work.'

Nathan narrowed his eyes. He had a sinking sensation he'd made a serious strategical error. 'What do you mean?'

'I've been a millionaire since I was twenty-two.'

He stared at her, trying to absorb this disclosure. A disclosure which could change everything for their future relationship. 'How?'

'I engineered a component and now I own the international patents. I sold the licence for a lump sum, and I also get a small pay-out for each component sold. It brings in a fair amount annually. I never used the money during my marriage; Dilip didn't want me to. I've left my annual income in the hands of some financial investment companies, and the initial licence capital has been sitting in savings accounts gathering interest for six years. I think I'll have enough resources to bring my child up adequately. Even if I don't have a job.'

The disdain dripping in those last sentences was palpable. Nathan was silent. He warred between intense admiration and pride in her accomplishment and shock. 'Why didn't you ever tell me?'

She shrugged. 'It didn't seem important.'

He blinked, trying to reassess the situation. If she didn't need him for financial security, what else could he use to convince her they should be married. He expelled a breath. He should have anticipated this wasn't going to be a quick, easy discussion. They needed to spend some more time together, so they could talk uninterrupted.

He ran a hand over his face. Work was hectic for the next few weeks and it would be Christmas soon. But Saira was right. They needed time to get to know each other again.

CHAPTER TEN

FOUR WEEKS LATER, Saira looked around her as she deboarded Nathan's plane at a private airstrip in the Alps.

Snow. He'd brought her to snow. Snow always held a magical quality for her. It had been years since she'd seen real snow. She'd missed it so much while living in Texas. His kindness warmed her heart.

She'd been hesitant when Nathan first suggested they take a getaway in the New Year to make decisions about the baby. Part of her had worried it was too early to be making decisions—but she knew she couldn't let her anxiety about the pregnancy prevent her from moving forward and making plans. She was trying her best not to let her worries about what could go wrong stop her from experiencing the joy of pregnancy.

'The roads to my chalet are clear,' Nathan said, resting his hand in the curve of her back to direct her. 'My SUV should be waiting outside. We can head there now, unless you want to get something to eat first.'

She shook her head. 'Chalet? So you don't have a Haynes resort here?'

'No. I did a feasibility study at one stage, but I think the ski industry is already well serviced in Europe. Ultimately I went in a different direction.'

Her excitement mounted as Nathan drove along the cleared roads edged by mounds of snow. He had large warm overcoats and fur-lined boots in her size in the boot.

She bit her lip. She wasn't going to well up at his thoughtfulness. She needed to keep her emotions under control for the difficult conversations they would inevitably have. But that was later. For now she would concentrate on what she'd do once she was outside, crunching in the snowfall.

The chalet was set back in the side of the mountain, but even with Saira's untrained eye she could see its position still allowed easy access to the slopes. There were fifteen other chalets in the area, but there was enough distance between them for privacy.

'Let me show you around,' Nathan said as he helped her down the from the car.

The chalet had a traditional Alpine design, with exposed beams and rustic stone features throughout. Almost every window provided a breath-taking view of the magnificent mountainous vista. The furnishings in the main living area were contemporary, as were the kitchen appliances, but the two en suite bedrooms had the rustic, chic charm she'd imagined for chalet living.

He put her suitcases in what was clearly the master bedroom, and carried his luggage to the smaller room.

Saira sat on a comfy sofa in her favourite area—a cosy snug off the main living room, with a log fire. It was a place where she could curl up with a mug of hot chocolate and a good book…

Although she wasn't here for indulgence but for a difficult and tense conversation.

She ran her hand across the slight swell of her stomach. She smiled. Each day the baby was growing a little bigger, a little stronger. And the need to make some decisions grew bigger too.

'What are you thinking?' Nathan asked, bringing her a cup of tea.

'Thinking about what your lawyers said.'

All of it seemed practical and sensible. Would Nathan accept one of the options offered instead since they would give him the same legal protection as if they were married. What would he get out of marriage that he wouldn't get from these other options?

She tried to see it from his perspective. The only difference was that he wouldn't live with the child. Why was marriage his preferred option when he would be spending so much time working anyway?

She realised she'd asked the question out loud when he replied, 'I want to be around whenever I'm not working. I'd prefer not to juggle my work travel and visitation dates. Marriage is the best solution. It also provides financial security and protection. It's a convenient arrangement.'

Saira heroically refrained from rolling her eyes. He wasn't answering the fundamental question—just concentrating on the work issue. Had she really expected anything different? 'Thanks, but I've already had one arranged marriage. I don't feel the need to have another one.'

He sat back. 'Your marriage to Dilip was arranged?'

'Yes.' She looked at him in surprise. 'I assumed you knew. I mean, it was the modern kind of arrangement. We were introduced by an aunty.'

'I didn't know you had an aunty.'

She grinned. 'An Indian aunty—no actual relation at all.'

'It wasn't love, then?'

'Not at first, but I knew I *could* love him when I agreed to the marriage, and I did grow to love him,' Saira said.

If she hadn't loved Dilip his death wouldn't have broken her. She didn't want to think about losing him. She wrapped her arms across her stomach. She didn't want to think about loss at all.

'What do you care anyway? You don't believe in love.'

'If you had an arranged marriage with Dilip, what's so different about marrying me?' Confusion was clear in his tone.

'Because Dilip wanted to get married. We were both actively looking for a lasting future. We believed we would grow to love each other, and we did. You don't think that's possible, do you?'

He dropped his head, obviously unable to meet her eye.

'So what you're suggesting is worse than an arranged marriage. With you, there's not even the possibility of feelings growing between us. What you're offering is cold and emotionless, and that's not what a marriage should be— definitely not when there's a child involved.'

She paused. She had assumed he was offering a real marriage, but perhaps that wasn't the case.

'Or are you suggesting we have a marriage of convenience only?'

'Marriage *would* be convenient. I've already said that.'

Saira sighed. 'I mean are you thinking we would have a marriage in name only?'

He raised his eyebrows. 'Name only?'

'Yes. Marriage for you to get your legal rights

but with no relationship between the two of us.'
She spelt it out for him. 'No sex.'

'No!'

She laughed at his emphatic response. Their
physical attraction hadn't gone away. If they
could have a relationship based on sex alone,
she had no doubt it would be successful. But she
already knew that wasn't possible. Her feelings
for Nathan were too strong.

She sighed as she looked through the large
window at the lights from the neighbouring windows, far enough away for them to have absolute privacy, but close enough to cast a magical
haze over the scenery.

'What's wrong?' Nathan asked.

'It feels strange.'

He raised his eyebrows in silent question.

'We're in this beautiful place. I'm surrounded
by snow.' She gestured widely with her hand.
'And we're here to discuss the future. We'll probably disagree a lot, because that's all we've done
so far.' She laughed humourlessly. 'It's a shame
I…we…won't get to enjoy it.'

He was silent for a few moments. She sighed.
Had she already spoilt the moment by voicing
her thoughts?

He came to stand next to her, putting his hand
on her shoulder. 'We're here for a week, Saira.
We don't have to start the serious discussions
straight away. If you want to take a few days to

enjoy the area that's not a bad idea. Maybe it will help us feel comfortable in each other's company again. I'm happy with that. Come on, let's take a walk round the chalets into the forest. There's a café on the other side which does excellent cheesy fries. Tomorrow perhaps we can wander round the village. They may still have the Christmas market stalls up, but there are plenty of shops there if not.' He paused. 'Unless you'd prefer to rest?'

Saira shook her head vehemently, desperate to get out into the white wonderland.

After visiting the café, where they shared a bowl of the most delicious fries Saira had ever eaten, they tramped through the snow around the chalets. Nathan looked on with an indulgent smile while she made a rudimentary snowman, giving her confidence to voice her secret wish.

'Really?' he asked, raising an eyebrow. 'You want to make a snow angel?'

'I haven't made one in years,' she replied, staring yearningly at the snow. It was so hard to resist the temptation to fling herself down.

'That's because you're an adult.'

In response, she stuck out her tongue and threw a snowball at him.

'That's not fair. I'm a gentleman. I can't retaliate.'

'A gentleman? Or are you being sexist?' She grinned as she spoke her challenge.

'I'm not going to throw snowballs at a pregnant lady.'

'Is that right?' She bent to gather more snow. 'Good to know.'

She threw snowballs in quick succession.

'Stop,' he protested with a laugh.

'Make a snow angel for me and I will.'

'*For* you? You want me to make the snow angel?'

'I'm pregnant.' She pressed a hand to her stomach. 'I don't want to risk hurting the baby if I fall backwards onto the snow. But I really want to see one.'

She opened her eyes and gave him her most pleading expression.

'You're doing this to see how far you can push me.'

'Not at all,' she protested, with a lack of conviction. 'One day our child will want to make snow angels. I'll be the cool, fun mum, right there, playing in the snow with them. Do you want to be the boring, humourless dad?'

'If that occasion ever happens I promise I will be in the snow too.'

He turned to head back inside, only stopping when another snowball hit him. She raised her hands in front of her face in the classic gesture of innocence.

'Come on, Nate. Just one snow angel. I think you should practise. You don't want to be a huge disappointment to your kid in the making snow angels department, do you?' She scrunched her nose. 'I'm only trying to help you.'

Her heart leapt as he laughed, the deep sound reverberating in her soul. He was far too serious at times. She could spend all her days trying to make him laugh.

She turned away to gather her thoughts. She needed to remember their relationship was because they were having a baby, not because of their feelings.

She turned back as he called her name—in time to see him fall back, then wave his arms and legs up and down.

Again, the tears welled up. Why did this kind, generous person believe he had nothing to give in a relationship? If only he would open himself up to the possibility love might develop between them they could have a chance at a real future. She wished she knew how to break through to him—she wished she had the right words.

To stem the flood of emotion, she took out her phone and snapped a picture. 'This one's going on social media.'

She grinned, stretching out a hand. He grabbed it, gently pulling her forward onto her knees.

She laughed. 'I should have expected that.'

He sat up, staring at her but saying nothing.

Their gazes locked. She couldn't break away, didn't want to do anything other than drown in those blue depths.

She licked her lips. The flare of awareness was an unwelcome intrusion. The rational part of her brain kept trying to remind her she needed to keep her distance, physically and emotionally, but every other part of her wanted to fling herself into his arms and bury herself in the warmth and security of his embrace.

If she was merely experiencing the old sexual attraction it wouldn't be such a problem; she could resist it. But the lid kept rising on the Pandora's box of her feelings and it was out of her control.

Vaguely she was aware of a cold, wet sensation in her knees. One of them needed to act—do something to release the charged atmosphere. Finally, she moved. Throwing herself into his arms, she pushed him back in the snow as her lips covered his.

Nathan already had the fire going when Saira came into the snug. She gave him a quick smile before taking a seat.

She hadn't said anything after their kiss. After he'd broken their connection they'd come inside, and she'd gone straight to her bedroom to change out of her wet snowsuit. He almost regretted ending the kiss, but it had flared quickly into desire and he had been moments away from making love to her right there in the snow.

Her expression was inscrutable as she thanked him for the hot chocolate, but at least there were no obvious signs of embarrassment.

'That shouldn't have happened,' she said. 'But it did.' She paused, drawing in a deep breath. 'And, let's be frank, we're still attracted to each other. It will probably keep happening.'

He grinned. Typical Saira—upfront and honest. It was refreshing how she owned her desire.

'What do you think we should do?' she asked.

His brows furrowed. He couldn't pretend the confirmation their sexual attraction was as strong as ever wasn't a huge advantage in his plan to convince her to marry him. But he was prepared to take this slowly, to bank down his sexual needs and give her the space to come round to his way of thinking.

He sat down next to her, turning slightly so he could look at her. Sex with Saira was wonderful, but the last thing he wanted was any resentment on her part. Not if they were going to have a real, true relationship together.

He went still at the thought. Was that what he wanted? A real relationship? Of course he did— but he meant sexually, not emotionally, particularly after what she'd suggested earlier.

'We need to decide this together,' he said.

She nodded in acknowledgement. 'I know, but

it's not a simple decision of whether we have an affair or not. Not this time. We have more than Miranda's wedding to think about.'

He nodded too. 'We're going to be parents soon. We're going to be part of each other's lives for the rest of our lives.'

She gave a harsh laugh. 'That's a grim prospect.'

He pursed his lips. If that was how she felt, he had his work cut out for him. 'It's reality. What we need to decide on is what else we'll be to each other.'

It wouldn't be a hardship to be married to Saira. And if he was getting married he wanted a physical relationship with his wife. He would be making a commitment to stay with her. He wasn't going to leave his family looking for sex outside the relationship. He wasn't his father.

His brow furrowed. Was that why she was so adamant she wouldn't marry him? Was she worried he would treat her like his father had treated his mother, ultimately abandoning her after a few years? He didn't blame her if those were her concerns. All he could do was prove to her he was a better man than his father.

Growing up, he had been proud when people compared him to his father, too young to notice all his flaws. Now he tried to distance himself from those comparisons. Even his preference for short-term relationships, ending them before they could get serious, was a reaction to his father, who had been constantly unfaithful during his marriage. It was better to end a relationship early rather than risk hurting someone, risk breaking their heart.

Nathan could promise Saira he wouldn't do the same. Marriage might not have been in his plans, but once he took his vows he would keep them. He needed to convince Saira of that.

He deliberately adopted a matter-of-fact tone. 'You know my preference.' He held up his hand as she opened her mouth to protest. 'But that's a separate discussion for another day.'

'It shouldn't be this hard,' she said with a rueful smile. 'All I wanted was a brief affair with an attractive man I really liked. And now look where we are. I don't want to rush into anything.'

She placed her hand across her stomach in a protective gesture. He might worry about whether he would be a good father after the baby was born, but she was worrying constantly already. It wasn't only about the future. She was anxious for this pregnancy. He understood why, based on her previous experience. He wished he could take her worry away. All he could do was be supportive while remaining positive—and make sure he didn't add to her worries.

'Part of the problem is you overthink things,' he said, reaching out to shake her knee gently. His hand rested there of its own accord.

On cue, she laughed in disbelief. 'Me? You do too.'

He shrugged casually. The best course of action was to keep things light between them. Sex didn't have to be a big deal. Not if they agreed boundaries. It had worked after they'd had the discussion in Gozo. There was no reason they couldn't come to a mutually satisfactory agreement this time too.

Although of course their initial agreement to keep their fling to their time on the island had gone out of the window once they'd continued their affair in London. Their physical attraction was special. He had never experienced the same with anyone else.

His mouth went dry as Saira reached out to put her mug on the low coffee table, the action tautening her jeans along her thighs, stretching her jumper across her full breasts. Hopefully that agreement would find her in his arms and in his bed.

'How about we let things happen for the time being?' he said. 'We've already agreed we'll spend a few days enjoying the area before we have a serious talk. Why don't we decide how we factor in our attraction then?'

'So, ignore it until then?'

'No, that's not what I meant at all.'

The warmth from the simple touch of his hand on her knee was spreading through him, providing a sense of ease and comfort rather than anything sexual at that moment.

'Why don't we enjoy this time together for the next few days, indulge this attraction? Later, when we discuss the baby, we can talk about whether we end it then, or continue for a limited time, or see how it plays out.'

'Go with the flow?' She quirked an eyebrow. 'That doesn't sound like you at all.'

'I'm not going to pretend I like this uncertainty, but you need to relax. Let's enjoy a few days without any talk of future plans, enjoy each other's company and see where our attraction takes us.'

He stared intently into her eyes, willing her to agree with his suggestion.

CHAPTER ELEVEN

SAIRA SAT CLOSE to the fire in the living room, sad that their brief holiday was already half over. Nathan was in the kitchen, preparing dinner, as he had every night so far.

He wasn't being subtle. He hadn't given up on the idea of them getting married, and there wasn't much he wouldn't do to get what he wanted. And she had to admit if she could make her decision based on his domestic skills alone they'd be in front of the registrar signing the marriage certificate as soon as they landed in London.

He hadn't argued with her decision to keep their relationship platonic. Tempted as she was to indulge their attraction, she wanted a clear head when they had their talk. She didn't want to be clouded by a sexual fug.

It hadn't stopped him flirting with her constantly. Which was fine. She was flirting outrageously back, and both of them were sneaking in quick kisses.

It was light and fun—like being a comfortable married couple.

She sighed. If they were a married couple it would be anything but comfortable. Much as she hated to end this idyllic time, they couldn't put off having their serious discussion much longer. The last couple of days had been a brief glimpse into what her world would be like if all her dreams could come true. But reality was always lurking, ready to intrude.

In an effort to distract herself she scrolled through messages and emails on her phone, smiling at an email from her mother with Indian wives' remedies for growing a healthy baby.

When she'd told her parents about her pregnancy over Christmas their reaction had taken her aback. Rather than being disappointed or concerned they'd both been overjoyed she was happy. She hadn't appreciated how worried they were about her since she'd lost her pregnancy and then Dilip died.

When they asked about the baby's father, it had been tempting to lie and pretend she and Nathan were together. In the end she wanted an honest relationship with her parents. She was strong enough to deal with the consequences of her actions and follow through on her decisions. They'd have to respect her independence.

They hadn't even blinked an eye when she explained the situation. They didn't know Nathan well, but they already loved Miranda, and were prepared to extend that love to her brother if he made their daughter happy.

She sighed. Sometimes it was hard to see that her parents' overprotective and disciplined approach to her upbringing was their way of loving her—a product of their own upbringing, not an attempt to assert control. She was learning there were many aspects of her past that she'd interpreted from an immature perspective. Including her relationship with Nathan.

Looking back from his point of view, she could see how her leaving him so soon after his father had abandoned the family contributed to his belief love and relationships were not meant to last.

She'd promised herself to stop dwelling on the past. She had to concentrate on the future—which included finding somewhere else to live.

After sending a quick reply to her mother, she checked her emails from estate agents. At the end of December her landlord had told her he was selling the flat and she needed to leave. So now she had to add house hunting on top of everything else she had to do to prepare for the baby.

Her hand cupped her slight but growing bump as she tried to download a file without success.

She walked through to the kitchen. Her glance took in the table setting, with flowers and candles, and she grimaced. If only she could make Nathan understand romantic gestures meant little unless there was true sentiment behind them. He cared about her. And because of that he would always look after her. But she wasn't interested in being taken care of. She was strong enough to take care of herself.

'What's up?' he asked.

'Can I use your laptop, please? Some estate agents have sent through a few particulars but I can't see them properly on my phone. I want to make appointments for viewings for when we get back home.'

He nodded. 'You mentioned you have to leave your flat soon.'

'Yes. But to be honest once I found out about the pregnancy I decided I want to buy a house. Somewhere with a garden, ideally.'

'Then you're staying in England? What about those job opportunities abroad?'

She pressed her lips together. It was curiosity, she reminded herself. He wasn't telling her where to live. It was irrelevant anyway.

'I'm putting my job hunt on the back burner for now. I don't know what the future holds, but I do know I want to be with our child while they're young. I feel blessed I have the choice. I put some feelers out about voluntary positions, so I can still contribute. We'll see,' she finished with a shrug.

'Any ideas where you'll live?'

'I was thinking, perhaps, looking in Buckinghamshire. I loved growing up there. And it's near your mum, and not too far from Ajay. It would be nice to be close to family. In an ideal world I would be able to buy before I have to move out, but there's such a shortage of houses available so who knows?' she said, flinging her hands up in the air. 'At least I don't have to worry about getting a mortgage, so I'm not going to complain about my first world problems.'

'You could stay at my place until you find somewhere.'

She reared her head. 'Really?'

'Of course. And we ought to discuss together where our child lives.'

Saira nodded slowly. 'I guess that makes sense… You'll want us to live close to London, so you don't have to travel too far for visits.'

'It's more than that. I meant what I said before. I would rather not have restrictions on when I can spend time with my kid. That's one of the reasons it would be best if we're married. I'm sure you don't want to be apart from the baby while he or she is with me, particularly if you're breastfeeding.'

Her mouth opened and she furrowed her brows. 'I hadn't really thought about it.' How had she not thought about that before? Deep anguish filled her at the realisation that unless she lived with Nathan her baby would regularly be away from her.

When she'd thought about Nathan seeing their baby, for some reason she'd imagined him in her house, spending time there. She hadn't for one moment thought the baby would be away overnight with him. How could she have been so naïve?

But now the reality of her future flooded through her mind. Periods of separation from her child. How many moments, how many milestones would she miss?

Nathan tilted her chin up with a questioning expression. 'Is something wrong?' he asked.

She shook her head giving him a wan smile.

'Dinner's almost ready. Do you want to use my laptop first?'

'No, it can wait,' she replied, taking a seat at the table.

Her thoughts were whirling, but until she had time to put them in order she didn't want to discuss them with anyone.

She took a mouthful of tender chunks of beef with perfectly cooked vegetables and groaned. 'This is delicious, Nate. Thank you.'

'You're welcome. How about a kiss for the chef?' he asked, bending towards her, his lips puckered.

She laughed before giving him a quick peck, then pushed his head away. She loved this light-hearted side of him. Why couldn't he admit he had feelings? Or allow the possibility that they could grow?

He did care about her—she could tell. If he would just try to give their relationship a chance to be loving and real—the way she had when she'd married Dilip—then they would both get what they wanted. But unless he admitted there was a chance he could love her it was hopeless.

And that was the crux of the matter. The real reason she didn't want to marry Nathan.

If he wasn't open to love growing between them he would feel trapped in their marriage. She would have to stand by every day knowing he desperately wanted to be free but was bound to her by his strong sense of honour and his need to prove he wasn't like his father.

He would come to resent her, and then, perversely, she would lose what mattered most. She would lose any chance of being loved, any chance at lasting happiness.

But if she didn't marry him she faced the idea of being separated from her baby for days and weeks at a time. The mere notion tore at her heartstrings. How had she been so foolish that she hadn't considered the reality of her child spending part of their time in a different house? For the first time she could understand why women married men they barely knew to ensure they would always be in their child's life.

She would consider all options if it meant not being separated from her baby. It didn't matter what the risk to her heart was. She sighed heavily. Why couldn't she have both?

Nathan sprayed whipped cream on the mug of hot chocolate, then added some marshmallows. He placed the mug on a tray next to a glass of orange juice and some breakfast pastries.

The previous evening Saira had been quiet over dinner and had then retired to her room. The discussions they needed to have were clearly weighing on her mind.

'Morning,' Saira said, coming into the kitchen area. 'Can I use your laptop later, please? I still need to email the estate agents.'

'Sure. I was about to bring you up some breakfast.' He gave her a bright smile which she didn't return.

She glanced quickly at the tray. 'Thanks, but I'm not hungry.'

'You didn't have much dinner last night either. It's not good for the baby if you don't eat properly.'

'Fine,' she said, perching on one of the kitchen

bar stools and pulling the tray towards her. Irritation crossed her face.

What had he said wrong now? Wasn't he supposed to be concerned for his child's wellbeing? He wasn't accusing her of anything.

Perhaps she was in a mood because she hadn't slept well. He thought he'd heard her pacing during the night.

She ate without speaking, deliberately concentrating on her phone.

'Ugh,' she groaned.

'What's up?' he asked.

'My mobile's reception here is terrible. Do you get a good signal? Can I use yours, please? I need to speak to Bastien.'

'Sure,' he said handing over his mobile.

Bastien? Why was she speaking to him?

She walked over to the window, where he couldn't hear her, but it was clear she was laughing. It wasn't jealousy he was experiencing, but her body language was completely relaxed as she chatted to Bastien. So different from the slight tension which was now present in their conversations.

'Is everything all right?' he asked when she returned.

Her smile dropped when she faced him. 'Yes. He says hello and he'll be in touch with you soon.'

'I didn't realise you and Bastien knew each other.'

Her eyebrows rose. 'We met on the holiday, remember?'

'I know. I meant I didn't realise you kept in touch.' It shouldn't bother him. He hoped it didn't sound as if he was bothered.

Saira frowned. 'I'm in touch with most of the people I met on holiday.'

'Why?'

'Why not? I liked them. I've met up with some of them individually a couple of times since we've been back. I'm surprised they didn't mention it, since you and I were together at the time. I haven't seen them since I found out about the pregnancy, though. I'm looking forward to seeing them at the Spring Ball. I should probably tell them about the baby, otherwise the big belly could come as a bit of a shock,' she said, giving him the first smile he'd seen from her that morning.

'The Spring Ball? I didn't know you were going to it.'

'I'm helping Bastien and his family with their foundation. They want to add a STEM element, so they've been liaising with Kent and me. I cannot believe Bastien's brother is an earl. I mean an honest to goodness peer of the realm. I almost curtseyed when we were introduced. No wonder Bastien sometimes hams up playing the part of the feckless spare to the heir so well.' She was silent for a moment. 'What is it? Have I done something wrong?'

'No, I wasn't aware you were in touch with my friends. That's all.'

How had he not known his friends had kept in contact with Saira? They never bothered to keep in touch with his other former girlfriends, thankfully.

'Don't worry. It's not going to interfere with your Six-Month Men Club. I'm their friend in my own right, not as your ex-girlfriend. I hope you don't have a problem with that,' she said, and then he caught the mumble under her breath. 'Not that it would matter to me if you *did* have a problem.'

His lips twitched. What a relief. The sass was back. His friends enjoyed wit and intelligent banter. Saira was exactly the kind of woman they'd like as a friend. And it would make their semi-annual get-togethers much better if they all got on well.

He tilted his head. The baby would only be a couple of months old in September. Perhaps Saira wouldn't want to travel.

He grinned. He was sure his friends would understand his reason for being the first one of them not to show up at their annual holiday. Hopefully, it would only be that first year, and after that Saira would be happy to join them with the baby. Then there would be family holidays with the three of them, or maybe four or more in the future…

An image of him in a swimming pool surrounded by Saira and their children came to mind. He was getting ahead of himself. He and Saira would have a practical marriage—it wasn't going to be like some romanticised family travel advert.

They still hadn't made any decisions.

'Would you like some coffee?' he asked holding up the pot. 'It's decaf.'

He grimaced. He hadn't realised how much he relied on caffeine to fuel him before he'd gone cold turkey in solidarity with Saira's pregnancy.

'No, thanks. The hot chocolate and orange juice are already more than enough for my bladder to handle.'

He glanced at her stomach, marvelling at the slight swell—a visible sign of his growing child. Ever since his father had left he never thought he would be a father himself, scared he was genetically incapable of being around for his children. But watching his baby grow a little each week was an experience he wouldn't want to miss.

The truth was his father hadn't been a presence in their lives for most of his childhood. His final abandonment had been more difficult for his mother and sisters to handle than it had for him. He would never do the same thing.

He frowned. Marrying Saira made the most

sense to him in this situation, but the reality was he had no concern she would restrict his time with his child. He had no doubts she would be generous with visitation and give him the same legal rights he would have if they were married.

And she had made it clear she was staying in the country. She wasn't planning to run away this time.

Could he honestly say he would have offered marriage to any woman who came to him with an unexpected pregnancy? He would have done the right thing, of course, so if any of his exes had become pregnant and wanted marriage he would have complied, but it wouldn't have been something he would insist on if he could have the necessary legal protections without it.

Why was he being so insistent with Saira? It wasn't simply because she was his sister's friend.

'We should talk,' he said abruptly.

'I know. I'm ready. Shall we go into the other room? We may as well be comfortable, and it will seem too formal if we talk over the table.'

They moved into the snug, sitting on separate sofas. The intimacy had already disappeared.

'We may as well dive in,' he said. 'You know my opinion. We get on well. I think we could have a successful marriage.'

'Based on what?' She raised her hands, shaking her head. 'I don't get this complete one-eighty you've done. You made it clear over and over that there was no future. You were adamant you don't do long-term commitment.'

'Things are different now.'

'Because there's a baby?'

'What other reason would there be?'

It wasn't a one-eighty. He still didn't believe marriages based on the romantic fiction of ever-lasting love would work. But a marriage based on raising a child, where there was also mutual respect and attraction, could be successful. He would work hard to make sure of it.

She rubbed her eyes. 'It doesn't matter what kind of marriage you're suggesting. I don't want to get married again. Not now, not ever. For me, having a child doesn't change the way I feel.'

He ran his hand over his face. For someone who claimed she'd once dreamed of a long-term future with him, getting married and having children together, she was showing great reluctance at the possibility of her dreams coming true.

He grimaced. He wasn't making her dreams come true, though—not really. She was a romantic at heart. She might have had an arranged marriage, but by her own words she had grown to love her husband. Her dream had never been for a loveless marriage—he couldn't offer her anything else.

He couldn't offer her love, or even pretend there was the possibility love would grow between them. Emotions were a weakness. Romantic love was a hormonal-induced illusion which didn't last.

He could try saying the words, if they would persuade her to marry him, but she would see through his deception which would make the situation worse.

He still had to make his case for a chance to have a real family.

'I think marriage is the best option for us.' He raised his hand before she could protest. 'I promise I'll keep an open mind while we talk about other options. As long as you promise to do the same about marriage.'

Saira furrowed her brows. He could see her wrestling with her thoughts before she gave a brief nod.

'At work, when we're trying to decide what action to take, we keep nothing off the table,' she said. 'All ideas are up for debate, nothing is too stupid. The only rule is we don't argue for or against until we've run out of ideas. Then we go to the evaluation phase. Perhaps we should approach this like that.'

'All ideas are on the table?'

'Everything—no matter how stupid.'

His lips twitched. If it kept marriage as an option he'd go with whatever method she proposed. How would she react if he suggested they use a SWOT analysis for their evaluation?

'Fine,' he said.

'Okay, then.'

Saira's smile warmed his heart.

She looked around, then walked away, coming back a few moments later with a paper and pens.

'The first option is to stay as we are. Stay separate, with a legal agreement to outline our arrangements.'

'Or we could get married.'

Saira rolled her eyes, but wrote on the paper. 'Perhaps we should outline what kind of marriage. We've already talked about having a platonic marriage of convenience.'

Nathan inhaled. He'd already discarded that notion, but he'd agreed nothing was off the table. 'That's one possibility. Or we could have a real marriage—with sex.'

'Well, I did say no idea was stupid at this stage,' she replied, writing it down.

He cleared his throat, trying to cover his laugh. 'Is that it, then? Some kind of marriage or continuing the way we are?'

Frankly, he didn't have much hope of them coming to an agreement during the holiday if those were the only options.

'We could have a time-limited marriage of convenience, so you could get your legal rights, and then we separate.'

'That is a possibility,' he said.

Not one he would agree to. If he got married he would be making a commitment and he would be staying married. He wouldn't be another Haynes male who couldn't make his marriage last. Like father, like son.

'I suppose my concern now is not being with the baby when it's your visitation time,' Saira said.

Marriage would take care of that. He nodded encouragingly.

'We could buy a place together,' she continued.

That was an unexpected suggestion. He turned the idea over in his mind. 'Live together, you mean?'

'Yes. Like housemates. I'm sure we could find a place big enough for us to live separate lives under the same roof. You could have the east wing and I could have the west wing.'

She giggled, and something intense flared through him.

'Or we could live together as a couple,' he suggested.

'You mean with sex?'

'Yes.'

'I don't know—'

'No stupid ideas, remember? Write it down.' He smiled watching her chew her lips as she wrote. 'Unless we have any more options, why don't I make us a drink and we can move on to evaluation,' he said, standing.

If he could convince her to live together as a couple it wouldn't be a far stretch to convince her to marry him. Then he would be able to do his duty to Saira and his child. And prove he wasn't like his father.

CHAPTER TWELVE

'I DON'T THINK we'll be able to buy a place before I need to move out of my flat,' Saira said, her dejection obvious. 'I guess I shouldn't complain. At least I have options. I can find somewhere to rent or move into my parents' place.'

They'd been back in England for almost a month. At the end of their Alpine holiday they'd agreed to buy a place together—live together but not as a couple. It was the solution she had hoped for. The only one that meant she wouldn't be separated from her child but Nathan wouldn't feel trapped, and she could remain hopeful that a real, loving relationship between the two of them might develop.

Since her return home, she'd spent every day she could going on house viewings. Nathan accompanied her when he was in town, but he'd been travelling most of the time.

There was one house she had fallen in love with immediately on viewing. It ticked all her boxes, and also included the non-essential extras

Nathan had mentioned, with its basement leisure and entertainment suite. But the extras took it out of her budgeted price. She'd only agreed to the viewing because Nathan wanted to get an idea of what was available at different price points. Which was a mistake—it set the bar too high for any other properties they'd seen since.

'Your mother also suggested I move in with her,' she said, glancing in his direction, wondering whether he would suggest she move in with him while they continued the search.

He was looking straight ahead, with a strange smile on his face.

She narrowed her eyes. 'What?'

He shook his head, pressing his lips together. 'I have a surprise for you.'

They were on their way to have lunch with Nathan's mother and sisters, taking the opportunity to show them the picture of their baby from the twenty-week scan the previous week. It was still unbelievable to her how clear the image of their daughter was.

She grinned. *Daughter.* They were having a girl. And if the scan was anything to go by she'd inherited her father's nose.

How was she already halfway through her pregnancy?

She rubbed a hand across her stomach. Her growing bump and the fluttering movements she was beginning to feel were a welcome sign her baby was growing and getting stronger. Part of her would always worry about this pregnancy, but every milestone she passed was a celebration for her.

There was still four months before the baby was due, but she felt unprepared. Did she even know how to be a mother to a girl? Loving her daughter and taking the best care of her weren't in question. But she wanted to be more.

Their daughter would love and admire her father—there was no doubt about that. But could she be a guide for her daughter? Someone she would look up to and be proud of?

She had to stop second-guessing herself. But this unknown territory terrified her.

She glanced over at Nathan, who still had a Cheshire Cat grin on his face. She'd missed him so much while he'd been travelling. But he wanted to take at least a month off once the baby was born; she couldn't fault him for that.

When they'd agreed to buy a place together it had sounded rational. She'd congratulated herself for getting Nathan to agree to her practical, if unorthodox, solution. But was it really a solution or was she being naive? Wasn't she risking more hurt and loss if Nathan did decide to leave her one day?

She'd asked herself the same questions over and over again and would probably continue to do so.

She wasn't sure how far she believed in Nathan's promise to keep marriage off the table—she suspected it might make a reappearance at any time.

She understood his need for the security of knowing he would be a real part of his child's life. She'd watched how he and Miranda had suffered the first time their father had left—even as a teenager he had a deep-seated desire not to be seen as like his father. She could even understand his need to create a family of his own—although she suspected he hadn't even admitted that was one of his reasons for asking her to marry him.

Was she even correct in thinking if Nathan was forced to marry her he would feel trapped and never learn to love her? Were his feelings more likely to grow if they stayed unmarried? She'd taken a chance with Dilip that he would come to love her—couldn't she do it again?

She mentally shook her head. No, that could only happen if Nathan was open to the idea that love and happily-ever-after existed. He hadn't said anything to show he had changed his mind about that.

They'd also come to a more formal agreement on the future arrangements for their daughter, including contingencies if things didn't work out.

And that was what her marriage to Nathan would be—a relationship with contingencies.

She didn't want that. She wanted a true relationship in which she could love openly, with all her heart. And be loved in return.

Nathan wasn't offering her that.

In all their discussions they'd concentrated on what would happen in the future. They still weren't talking about the past, about the problems that had driven them apart—although it was clear the resentment, the blame, was still a sore point for him. For both of them. Until they did talk about that, any real future together wasn't a possibility.

The sudden quiet stillness made her realise the car had stopped and the engine was turned off. He turned to face her, reaching across the gearstick to cover her hands.

'Well,' he said. 'Here we are.'

They were in front of her dream house. Her smile faltered. 'Why are we here? We've already viewed this house.'

'You loved it—be honest.'

'Of course. It's perfect, except it's too expensive. We already discussed this.'

What was he thinking? Why did he look so pleased?

He shrugged. 'Come on,' he said, getting out of the car and coming round to open her door. 'Come with me.'

He took a set of keys from his jacket pocket and opened the front door.

'Surprise!' he said, with a large smile on his face as he threw his arms wide.

Saira gave a smaller smile, looking round the hall in bewilderment.

'I don't understand,' she said. 'What's the surprise?'

'This,' he replied, gesturing round.

'This house?'

He nodded, beaming.

'You bought it?' she asked in disbelief.

Nathan laughed. 'No, of course not. I know you have this ridiculously strange desire to be involved in the conveyancing process. I wasn't going to deprive you of that joy.' He tapped her nose affectionately. 'No. I rented it.'

She shook her head. 'I need to sit down.'

She walked into the lounge area, noticing the furniture in place. When they'd viewed the property it had been empty, the owners having moved out already.

'What's happened? Where did all this come from?' she asked, pointing to the furniture.

'I rented that too. If you don't like anything we can easily replace it. Either buy new stuff or rent something different. Up to you. I didn't want you to come into an empty house.'

The last thing she'd expected this morning was for Nathan to have rented the house she loved.

'How did this happen? I didn't know it was available for rent.'

He gave her a pointed look.

'Oh, I see,' she said with dawning understanding. 'Money talks.'

'I made them an offer they couldn't refuse.' He waggled his eyebrows. 'I've rented it for a year with an option to buy.'

She laughed at his playfulness. 'Why? Why would you go to that trouble?' she asked.

'Because you love this house. And you were getting stressed about not having somewhere to move to. I know you're worried about tempting fate by doing things too early for the baby. Renting was the perfect solution to all those issues.'

Saira covered her mouth. How had he known? The first time she'd voiced her concern about not finding a place had been in the car earlier. And she *had* been reluctant to commit to large purchases or finalise things for the baby. How had he picked up on that?

She would do anything to keep this Nathan around—not the stern, serious man he often presented to the rest of the world. This Nathan, with his generous heart and cheerful, carefree manner. She wanted a relationship with this Nathan.

'Saira…' His voice broke softly into her thoughts. 'Is everything all right?'

Saira gulped. 'Everything's perfect. This is perfect.' She stood up, walked over to him, and threw her arms round his waist—or as far as she could reach with her protruding bump getting between them. 'Thank you.'

'You're welcome,' he replied, kissing the top of her head. 'I'd do anything for you and our baby—you know that.'

Saira was unable to say anything, reluctant to break away from his enveloping warmth.

After a few moments he gently pulled away. 'Come on, my mum's expecting us. We should head off.'

They arrived at his mother's house within half an hour and went straight into the dining room for their meal.

Lunch with Nathan, his mother and his sisters was always an entertaining occasion. Miranda and Steve had also come up for the day. Naturally, most of the focus was on the baby, the scan photos, and Nathan's surprise house rental.

Saira had a broad smile perpetually on her face as she watched the family interact. Her baby was lucky to be a part of this close-knit group. She studied Nathan's profile as he listened intently to his sisters. His expression was soft and there was an indulgent half-smile about his lips.

There was no doubt in her mind he would make a loving, involved, if somewhat overprotective, father. He was the kindest, most caring, most thoughtful person she knew.

It was one part of the complex tapestry that made up the man she was in love with.

She inhaled sharply, her eyes widening.

She was in love with him. Of course she was. Why else had she been worried about a loveless marriage?

She didn't *want* to love him. Had tried to stop herself. Convince herself she wanted to be independent. Love meant losing control. Love meant loss, and she'd already lost so much—her baby, Dil… She'd even lost Nathan once before.

But it didn't matter. She loved Nathan.

They were having a baby together. They were going to live together. If she reached out and told him how she felt, perhaps he would start believing that long-lasting love was possible. Perhaps they could work through the past. Perhaps he would be open to the idea that he might come to love her. And perhaps they could have a real future together.

The possibility was terrifying.

She tuned back in to the conversation in the middle of Beatrice telling them a story about something that had happened to her on the internet.

'I think you need to be careful,' Nathan said to his sister when she'd finished her story. 'It all sounds a bit fishy to me.

'Yeah, that's what Dad said too,' Beatrice replied.

* * *

Nathan reared back, his entire torso stiffening. Keeping his voice quiet and steady, he asked, 'What did you say?'

Beatrice stared at him defiantly—an expression he hadn't seen on his sister since her rebellious teen years.

'Dad got in touch with us,' Beatrice explained. 'He wanted to meet with us and we wanted to meet with him. So we did. He wants to be back in our lives.'

Back in their lives. Just like that. After eight years his father had waltzed back into his sisters' lives. Probably not caring about the damage he would do.

He clenched his fist. A warm hand covered it, giving it a gentle squeeze. He looked at Saira while he tried to gather his whirling thoughts.

Why was his father back? What did he want?

And his sisters didn't seem to have any problem in agreeing to meet him. Had they forgotten how he'd abandoned them when they were younger? Didn't they remember the nights they spent crying in Nathan's arms, asking him why their daddy didn't love them any more?

'Why?'

A simple question, but he needed answers to many different whys.

Why had his father returned? Why now? Why was he disrupting their carefully rebuilt lives after so many years? Why were his sisters letting their father back in their lives? Why weren't they worried his father would turn his backs on them again? Why didn't they care how Nathan felt—after everything he tried to do for them? Why didn't they care how much meeting their father would hurt Nathan? *Why?*

'He wants to get to know us,' Beatrice said.

'He hasn't cared about that for years.'

'That's not true, Nathan,' his mother said.

He turned to focus his attention on her. 'What do you mean?' he asked.

'He tried to keep in touch after he went to Australia, but he knew it upset me so he didn't push it. And I honestly believed it was better for the girls not to be torn between us. But he's asked a few times every year. He told me he's tried to contact you and Miranda on a number of occasions, but you've rebuffed him.'

'Did he expect me to welcome him with open arms?'

His mother glanced at her plate, her hand playing with the stem of her wine glass. 'When Juliet turned eighteen I said it was her choice, and she and Beatrice both decided to see him.'

'I see. It doesn't bother you he's back?' he asked his mother.

'I'm fine with it—honestly, Nathan,' his mother replied. 'What about you? Do you think you'll meet your father while he's in the country?'

'I don't think so.'

He had nothing to say to the man. Juliet and Beatrice might be ready for a relationship with their father, but he knew better. His father was fickle—his love for his family nothing but a transient emotion. Nathan suspected any warnings he tried to give would fall on deaf ears.

He sighed internally. If he couldn't protect his sisters from hurt, then he would have to be ready to comfort them when his father walked away again.

He turned to Miranda, who hadn't said much so far. 'Has Dad been in contact with you?'

His sister's inability to meet his eyes gave him her answer. He closed his eyes, lowering his head. She'd lied to him too.

He took a deep breath, looking round the table at his family. 'I'm sorry I made you feel you couldn't tell me you were meeting with him.'

'I didn't know how I would feel until I did.' Miranda took a deep breath, grasping Steve's hand. 'I know it was hard when Dad left. The last time particularly. You were there for us— you stepped in as a father figure even though you were barely an adult yourself. I understand why you don't want to be in contact with Dad. But over the last few years I've been thinking about Dad a lot. Especially after I started falling for Steve. I've wanted to meet Dad for a while. I hope you understand, Nathan.'

He was trying hard to understand, but out of his whole family keeping their father's return from him, Miranda's secrecy felt the most like betrayal.

He loved all his sisters—would do anything for them. But he and Miranda had always been particularly close. There was a large age gap between them and Beatrice and Juliet. Miranda had been only ten when their dad had left the first time. Nathan looked after her when their mother was unable to, trying to make up for his father's absence.

Now she had hidden this meeting from him.

'Nathan,' Miranda said. 'I want to invite Dad to my wedding.'

He took a forceful breath, trying to calm the blood rushing through his head. He pasted on a smile. 'It's your wedding, Miranda. You should invite whoever you want to invite. You don't need to check with me.'

They discussed the wedding arrangements for a while, with talk of their father seemingly forgotten, until Juliet said with a grin, 'Maybe Dad can walk you down the aisle, Miranda.'

Miranda laughed, but didn't say anything to contradict her. Nathan hoped his face didn't show his shock. Perhaps it made sense that a daughter wanted her father to perform the traditional role. But his sense of betrayal was stronger than ever.

'It's odd you don't want to meet Dad,' Beatrice said. 'Particularly now you're going to be a father yourself. I think you'd get along well. You're exactly like him.'

Although he'd heard people say that for years, the comparison was a bitter pill that day, Finding out his mother and sisters had been lying, keeping secrets from him—excluding him from their lives. Hearing they were ready to welcome a man who'd walked out on them before. A man who'd already proved he couldn't be trusted. A man who had never been there when they'd needed him. A man they couldn't depend on.

Was that really how his family saw him too? Like that man?

He'd given up so much for his family. Changed his plans so he could stay around for them. Lost his relationship with Saira. And they thought he was exactly like the man who'd abandoned his family without a backward glance.

A small squeak from Saira brought him back to the present. He loosened his grip on her hand. He took a deep, shuddering breath and tried to concentrate on the ongoing conversation.

The drive back to Saira's apartment was made in silence. He ignored Saira's efforts to initiate a conversation. He didn't want her pity—or, worse, her justifications for his family's decision to hide their meetings with his father. In the end she dozed off.

He'd never expected to be a father, and his instinct to be there for this child had been so strong it had overpowered his rational common sense. For a brief moment he'd thought he could be the kind of parent his father never was. But past was prologue. He couldn't do long term and he would be a fool to convince himself otherwise.

He *was* like his father. Everyone said it. As much as he would like to deny it, he had to accept it was true. Like his father, he didn't know how to commit. He couldn't take a chance on hurting his child the way his sisters had been hurt.

He would hurt Saira too. Perhaps she didn't care for him yet, but she would eventually—particularly if he persuaded her to restart their physical relationship. It was in her nature to care, to love wholeheartedly. He would inevitably hurt her the way he had before.

He could finally admit it to himself—the reality he'd been refusing to acknowledge for years. Despite their youth, Saira had developed strong feelings for him in the past. She'd loved him then. He'd pulled away and it had broken her heart. Despite his best intentions, in trying to spare her feelings and not wanting to give her false expectations he'd ended up doing the one thing he never wanted to do.

He'd hurt her deeply.

Maybe as deeply as his father had hurt his mother.

Wasn't he about to repeat the same behaviour? Promising Saira something based on the best intentions but knowing it wasn't something he could truly deliver. What if he really was like his father and would walk out on his family some time in the future. He wanted to commit to them, but he could he, from the bottom of his heart, make that promise?

He could potentially hurt Saira much more in the future if he tried to stay a part of her life. And, worse, this time he would also hurt their daughter. He couldn't put them through that. He wanted to believe he was a better man, but he wouldn't risk hurting Saira or his daughter. He wouldn't risk breaking their hearts when he couldn't live up to their expectations.

Far better not to be there at all than to break their hearts somewhere down the line. Far better to do it now, before he caused her more pain.

Something shifted inside him as he closed the doors around the possibility of raising the daughter he already loved. It was the hardest decision he would ever have to make. But walking away now was the best thing for her—and for Saira.

He parked outside Saira's place, then shook her gently awake. She gave him a sweet smile which twisted his heart.

'Saira, we need to talk.'

She blinked a couple of times, as if trying to clear the sleep away. 'Sure, do you want to come up?'

He shook his head. 'I think you and the baby will be better off if I'm not part of your lives.'

'What?' she asked with a disbelieving laugh.

'I'm only going to hurt you and her in the long run. I'll provide financial support, naturally. But I don't think we should live together. I don't think it's sensible for me to be part of her life while she's growing up. It's too big a risk. Perhaps when she's older she can decide whether she wants to know me.'

Saira scrunched her forehead. 'I don't understand. What risk? We shouldn't talk about this in the car. Why don't you come up and we can discuss this properly?'

'There's nothing to discuss. I won't be responsible for breaking her heart.'

'I don't understand,' Saira repeated. 'Where is all this coming from? You're not making sense. The whole point of all this, and us looking for a house together, is so you can be there for your child. So that we can both be.'

'I thought that was the best solution, but I was wrong. Our girl will be better off without me in her life at all rather than have me float in and out when I have time for her. I saw what that did to my sisters and my mother.'

Saira turned to him, shock in her eyes, 'You would never do that.'

'I wish that was true, but I can't guarantee it. I'm too much like my father. As much as I hate it, it's true. I understand now why you don't want to marry me. I'm a bad risk. I hurt you in the past, and you're rightly worried I'm going to hurt you both by abandoning you and the baby.'

'That's not it at all. Look, Nathan... I get the news of your father has come as a huge shock, but there's no need to overreact. Of course it would be better if our daughter grows up with you in her life.'

He stiffened at her implication he was over-reacting. He was doing the best thing for his daughter and for Saira. 'You're wrong. Miranda, Juliet and Beatrice, even my mother, were all better off when my father left once and for all.'

Saira opened her mouth, but then closed it. He swallowed under her intense scrutiny and turned to face forward, concentrating heavily on the car parked in front. She sighed deeply. He sensed her nodding a couple of times before she opened the car door. He turned to the side as he felt cold air come through the open door.

She leaned in. 'I don't think you're going to listen to anything I have to say at the moment. But I know you will be there for us. I trust you. I hope you change your mind, Nathan. I hope it for your sake and our baby's.'

She closed the door.

Why did she trust him? All the evidence showed to the contrary. He was his father's son. She was wrong to trust him.

He watched as she walked to her apartment building, resisting the temptation to go after her. As she entered the code she rested her other hand on her growing bump. He sucked in a breath. It would kill him not to be able to watch his daughter grow up. It would kill him to stay away from Saira—not to talk to her, not to hear her laugh, not to hold her in his arms.

But he was doing the right thing. For them—if not for him. He had to walk away before anyone else got hurt.

CHAPTER THIRTEEN

IT HAD BEEN two weeks since Nathan had dropped his bombshell announcement. Saira waited for him to contact her, tell her he'd made a mistake, changed his mind. Nothing.

With no scans or doctor's appointments on the horizon, in the end she'd messaged him, asking for the keys to the rental house. Now she was standing outside the property, waiting for them to be brought round.

She was trying to empathise with his situation. It must have been devastating to find out from his sisters that his father was back in their lives. Worse to realise they'd kept it from him. She didn't blame him for his reaction. She was sure once he'd had the chance to process things he would see there was no comparison between his father and himself, and he would want to carry on with their plans to move in together.

Why couldn't he talk about how he was feeling with her instead of closing himself off and shutting her out? Every time she wanted him to turn to her, to show her he needed her, he turned away instead.

Her heart literally hurt as her dreams of the future crashed before her.

It didn't even make any sense. Nathan couldn't simply drop out of their lives. She was his sister's best friend. They would always be seeing each other.

She couldn't believe he really meant to stay away. She didn't want to believe it.

Perhaps she was fooling herself, but the fact that Nathan had spoken impulsively, that he hadn't had time to process or think things through rationally, so this wasn't the most level-headed decision, perversely gave her a glimmer of hope that there was still a way forward for them together.

Or perhaps she needed to accept they weren't meant to be together. They'd already tried so many times, and each one of those times had created a ghost that haunted their interactions in the present.

She'd bounced between extreme emotions countless times over the past couple of weeks. She had to know one way or another. She couldn't carry on living in this limbo land of half-hope, half-despair.

Each time they said goodbye she never really believed it was the final time. Even when she'd left for the States, thinking her relationship with Nathan was over, she hadn't been able to imagine feeling strongly for another man. She never wanted to experience those lows again. Initially relationships of any kind weren't on her agenda. Her total focus had been on her work and studies.

Looking back at that time through the lens of maturity, pursuing an arranged marriage had only become an attractive proposition after she'd read a gossip article about Nathan and the women he was dating. The realisation he had moved on had been the final sign that she needed to move on as well.

Calm, quiet Dilip had been the perfect antidote after the intensity of her relationship with Nathan. She'd cared for him when they'd married and truly believed love would develop over time. Her devastation when Dilip had died was a clear sign she had grown to love him, making her more determined never to expose herself to that kind of loss again.

Her need to be independent and stand on her own two feet was a way to protect herself. Closing her heart to love and romance was meant to close her heart to pain. Unfortunately, she was learning the hard way that when it came to love, in a war between head and heart, the head rarely won.

She loved Nathan—deeply, completely, enduringly.

She could be independent and raise her daughter on her own if she needed to. It wouldn't change the way she felt about Nathan. Even though loving him meant opening herself up to the possibility of loss.

And she needed to accept part of the blame. Had her refusal to marry him contributed to his belief he was untrustworthy?

He didn't believe in love or lasting commitments because of the way his father had walked out on his family. Hadn't she exacerbated his belief when she'd gone to the States? Run away when he needed her the most? If she had spoken to him before she left—explained how she felt, what she hoped for their future—might there have been a different outcome?

Didn't she owe it to him—and to herself—to be honest now? Instead of hiding her true feelings she needed to tell him what she wanted—a real, loving relationship. Or at least the chance of one in the future. She'd taken that chance before, when she had her arranged marriage, she could do it again.

If only she could convince him to open his heart to the possibility of love growing between them. That would be enough for her. She didn't expect him to love her now. That was fine—she had enough love for all of them. All she needed was the mere possibility they could have a loving relationship in the future.

Her head turned as she heard a car pulling into the driveway. She didn't recognise the vehicle, but there was no doubt Nathan was driving.

He'd come.

He didn't have to come. He could have sent a courier with the keys. His presence had to mean something.

Maybe she was going to go down in flames. She didn't care. She wasn't scared of demanding what she wanted any more. She had nothing to lose and the chance of gaining something wonderful.

Her heart sank when Nathan walked towards her. Stiff. Grim. Unyielding.

He let them into the house, then deactivated the alarm. 'Keys,' he said as he handed them over.

'Thank you.'

'A car's coming to take me to the airport soon. Is it all right if I wait here until it arrives?'

'Of course,' she replied as they walked through to the open plan kitchen-living area. 'But what's going to happen to the car you came in?'

'Oh, yes.' He reached into his pocket. 'I've leased that car for you. I didn't want you staying here without any transportation and I know you can't borrow a family car. Again, if you don't like it you can lease something else.'

Tears pricked behind her eyes. He was always trying to find ways to make things easier for her. Was it any wonder she loved him?

'Oh, I nearly forgot.' He walked out of the house, then came back with a couple of grocery bags. 'I picked up a few things. I didn't know whether you would have time to shop before you got here.'

She bit her lip, blinking rapidly as she fought against her instinct to hug him. Any child would be lucky to have this wonderful, caring man as their father. He cherished the people he cared about.

She loved him. She had to let him know— even though she would be exposing herself to more hurt. It would be worth it for the chance of the future she wanted. She had to lay everything on the line.

Could she do it? Would he turn away? Would he reject her? Would he break her heart again?

She stood up straight, her shoulders back. She was strong enough to deal with that if it happened.

'Me not wanting to get married was never about you. It was about me,' she blurted out.

He stiffened 'It's okay. You have every reason to think I won't be a good husband.'

'No. That's not it. I wanted to be independent.

To prove I could bring up a child on my own if I had to. I've already lost so much in my life—Dilip, a baby, even you. I didn't want to risk getting hurt again.'

'I understand. I've hurt you so many times before and I would only hurt you both in the long run. You deserve better.'

She tutted with frustration. She was saying this all wrong. 'That's not true. You wouldn't hurt us.'

He walked over to the windows, staring out at the garden. 'You don't know that.'

'I *do* know,' she said with complete conviction. She needed to make him believe he was capable of commitment—that he was trustworthy.

He turned suddenly, a questioning look on his face.

'You're always there for the people you care about,' she began. 'You've always been there for your mother and your sisters. I can see how much you love them. You can't have any doubts about how much they love you. That's probably why your sisters are so open to knowing your dad.'

His brows creased. 'What do you mean?'

'You gave them everything they needed. You did everything for your family. You looked after them. You supported them. You protected them.'

Was anything she said getting through to him? She couldn't stop now.

'They never lacked for a father figure growing up because of you. They have no reason to resent your dad for not being there because *you* were instead. That's why I know you're going to be the most amazing dad.'

When he didn't respond, she continued.

'Look at what you've already done for us. You rented this place. You leased a car. You made sure we would be safe. You even brought food.'

'That's nothing.'

'That's not nothing. You didn't have to do that. Your father would never have done that—it wouldn't even cross his mind. Your father was a selfish man. The only person he cared about was himself. With every action you show how different the two of you are. You are nothing like him.'

She swallowed when he shook his head. The scars of his father's actions ran deep within Nathan. Her heart ached at his mistaken belief they were in any way similar.

'You know, I've been worrying a lot recently,' she said. 'Not only about the house or our living arrangements. I worry about the pregnancy. I worry about looking after the baby when she's born. I worry about whether I'll make a good mother. And it's not going to stop. I'm going to be a mum. I know I'm going to worry about my child for the rest of my life. But I've never—not for a moment—worried about you leaving us.'

There was still no obvious reaction from him. He just stood there, watching her.

'I'm not worried you will abandon me or our daughter. I have never once thought that. I have always known you will do everything you can to be part of our child's life. I don't believe there is any risk of you leaving us. I trust you, and if it takes marriage to convince you then we can get married.' She inhaled deeply. 'I love you, Nate.'

She held her breath, willing him to speak.

His phone beeped. 'The car's here. I have to go,' he said.

Her jaw dropped. That was all he had to say.

She'd done everything she could. All she could do was watch him walk out the door. Her shoulders slumped. She put herself out there, risking her heart, and now she was left alone with her dashed hopes.

Nathan glanced out of the window of the hospitality facilities in the private hangar where his plane was sitting on the Tarmac. He was due to board within fifteen minutes, then he'd be in New York for three or four days at least.

He tried to concentrate on the legal papers in front of him. If he couldn't get his act together it was pointless him even going to this meeting. The last thing he needed to deal with was a potential hostile management issue when there was something more important to sort out back at home.

Some*one* more important.

He frowned. When had Saira become the most important person in his life?

He admired her forthright attitude. He was fascinated by how her mind worked. He respected her opinions. He trusted her.

He inhaled sharply. If that was the case—if he trusted her—why was he finding it hard to believe what she was telling him now?

She'd always believed in him. Believed he would be there for the baby. For her. In her mind there had never been any shadow of a doubt he could be a good father and a stable presence in his child's life. How did she have so much faith in him?

He replayed their conversation. She was right. He loved his mother and his sisters. Even though he was hurt, felt betrayed when he heard they were in contact with his father, he was and always would be there for them. He already loved his daughter and would always be there for her. He would never abandon them. He wasn't like his father.

Saira was right and he would always be there for her too.

Because he loved her.

Saira was his priority. She always would be.

Not because of the baby but because she was Saira.

He was an idiot. Too blind to see what was patently obvious.

In his early twenties, his father's abandonment had caused him to doubt love existed. He dealt with that by pushing away people he cared about, not trusting that forever was possible.

When Saira had run away soon afterwards— when he pushed her away—he'd become convinced he wasn't capable of loving anyone. But that wasn't true. Far from being someone who didn't believe in love, he'd loved once and it lasted a lifetime.

The media dubbed him one of the Six-Month Men because he didn't have any relationship lasting longer than six months. But they'd got one major thing wrong. It wasn't because he was incapable of commitment that none of his relationships were long term. It was because nobody could come close to the woman he'd given his heart to years before.

He loved Saira. Had always loved her. He'd loved her years ago with the passion of youth. He loved her now with a depth borne of time, distance and maturity. Even after all these years he'd never stopped loving her. He never would.

And she loved him.

They would always be in each other's lives.

Tied to each other not only because of the baby but because they loved each other.

He laughed at the simplicity of his realisation, eager to return to her—to tell her how he felt.

If it wasn't too late.

He'd almost let it all slip away by not believing in himself. By walking away before he could cause pain to the people he loved. The legacy of his father had burrowed deep.

He would need to have an open and honest conversation with his family about his father's return. His father's actions had far-reaching consequences beyond the pain he'd inflicted on his family. It almost cost Nathan the love of his life.

Perhaps he would arrange to meet his dad—there were clearly things that needed to be said. But right now his priority was to get back to Saira.

With his usual efficiency and determination he rearranged his flight, discussed the complex issues which would need to be resolved at the New York meeting with the employees who would cover his absence, and called his driver back.

Perhaps he should send a text to Saira? He got out his phone, then hesitated. What would he write? If he told her he was on his way back she would worry about the reasons. He didn't want her to worry. But he couldn't give her an explanation yet. What he wanted to say was too important for a text message.

He paced around the hangar until he was finally in his car, heading out of London. If his driver was giving him curious glances, unused to his employer changing his mind about anything, Nathan didn't care. He leaned against the car seat, closing his eyes, mentally rehearsing what he was going to say.

Abruptly he opened his eyes again.

There was no planning this. If he wanted to tell her what was in his heart, he could only speak from his heart.

No matter how it went today, the baby was a connection between them, and he would reassure her his devotion to the baby wouldn't alter even if she told him she never wanted to see him again.

He already loved their daughter, but at first he'd grasped at the pregnancy as an excuse to stay in Saira's life.

If only he hadn't proposed to her in such a pragmatic fashion. No wonder she believed the reason he'd asked her to marry him was because he wanted to do the right thing for their child. The baby had nothing to do with his insistence on marriage anyway. Their child was a tie binding them together irrevocably—marriage wouldn't change that.

Despite what he rationalised, the simple fact was he'd proposed because he wanted to spend the rest of his life with Saira. He needed her; she was the missing piece which made him whole.

Marriage was too important for her to agree to it for the sake of the baby. She would never treat it as a legal tool the way he'd suggested. It was in her nature to put her heart and soul into her family, and he couldn't offer anything less than the same. Her offer to marry him earlier showed how much faith she had in him.

His driver made good progress and they were soon driving up the road to the house.

Nathan ran a business empire. Thousands of people relied on him for their livelihoods. He liaised regularly with royalty and politicians. But nothing was more nerve-racking than the moment the car pulled in through the gates of the house.

'Is something wrong? Aren't you flying to New York?' Saira asked as he entered the house. Her hand reached out, but she brought it down and gathered the fabric at the side of her dress.

That was a good sign, wasn't it? She was concerned about him. That had to mean he hadn't ruined everything by leaving.

'I am. I will be. They can handle things without me for a few days,' he replied.

'Okay. Would you like a drink?' she asked, leading the way to the living area.

He shook his head. 'I'm fine.'

Now he was in front of her he didn't know where to start. He took a deep breath. These were probably the most important words he would ever say.

CHAPTER FOURTEEN

SAIRA BRACED HERSELF, hoping her face wasn't showing the signs of her tears. Why was he here? Why was he back? Why was he looking so nervous?

'Saira.' He cleared his throat.

'Nathan.'

'I'll always be here for you.'

'I know, Nathan.'

She smiled weakly. He didn't have to come all the way back here to tell her, although it was reassuring—if not a little surprising.

'I've never doubted you would be here for the baby. I'm glad you believe it yourself now,' she said.

'Not only for the baby. Of course I want to be part of our child's life. Of course I do. But it's more than that. I'll always be there for you too.'

She took a sharp intake of breath. What did he mean, he would always be there for her? She was trying not to read too much into his words.

He shrugged. 'We were too young to start dating when we were at school. I think we both knew that. But there was still something between us. When you started university I moved to London so I could be there too. I wanted us to be together when you were in your first year, but I waited until you had at least a year to experience university life before I contacted you.'

Her eyes widened. She hadn't known he'd planned that. When she'd started university she'd hoped Nathan would contact her—keeping tabs on what he was doing through Miranda. Even entering her second year, no man could hold her interest. She'd thought her dreams were coming true when he finally asked her to meet him. She hadn't realised he'd waited to give her space to experience university life—putting her needs above his.

He continued, 'I knew you would be spending a year abroad in the States. My plan was to open a satellite office in the same area, so I could still be there with you.'

She opened her mouth but no words came out. She blinked heavily, trying not to let her emotions run wild. Trying not to interrupt. He needed to get this off his chest.

'When we argued, and you left, I was going to follow but my family needed me. I had to stay here. Then you got married. Although I would still have been there if you ever needed me, I

knew there wasn't any realistic chance of that—
so I put my effort into growing a successful
business. I convinced myself I wasn't capable
of caring for somebody enough to make a commitment.' He shrugged. 'Somehow I knew there
would never be anyone else for me. That's why
no other relationship had any chance of lasting.
When you came back, I couldn't believe we had
another chance. I'm sorry I blew it. I'm sorry I
turned my back on you after lunch with my mum
and sisters. I didn't trust myself—didn't trust that
I could be there for you. But I trust you. And you
trust me.'

His tense expression faded as his mouth widened in a grin.

A cocktail of jumbled thoughts mingled with
the avalanche of emotions rooting Saira to the
spot. She stared at him, her knees giving way as
she stumbled for the sofa. He could have warned
her she would need to sit down for his declaration.

For someone who measured every word and
never spoke more than necessary, Nathan's hastily spoken speech, tripping over the words to
get them out, showed her the depth of his feelings more clearly than what he hadn't quite got
round to saying.

'Saira?' he said, his voice low and uncertain.

'You said you'll always be there for the people you love,' she said in a soft tone.

He nodded. 'Yes.'

'And you said you'll always be there for me.'

'Always.'

'That sounds like you might love me,' she suggested hesitantly.

'Of course I love you. I always have.'

The simplicity of his words opened the floodgates, and she convulsed with the emotional impact of the declaration she'd longed for so long to hear. He took a step towards her, then stopped. She looked up, giving him a tremulous smile. He smiled as he gathered her in his arms, holding her close while she tried to compose herself.

Finally she met his gaze fully, unflinchingly. 'Why have you never told me before?'

'I thought actions spoke louder than words,' he replied, wiping the tears off her cheeks.

She laughed, and sniffed. 'I need the words too.'

He rubbed his chin. 'I love you.'

The words were stark. Simple. There was no doubting their sincerity.

With a startled exclamation she put her hand over her stomach.

'What's the matter? Are you in pain?' he asked with immediate concern.

'No,' she replied, with wonder in her voice. 'I

definitely felt the baby move that time. I think your daughter likes hearing the words as well.'

She took her hand in his and placed it where she'd felt the movement. They sat close together in perfect harmony, experiencing the faintly discernible movements of their child.

Without saying a word they let their lips meet—tender, loving, with an undercurrent of the passion that inevitably flowed between them.

'Does that mean you still love me?' he asked.

'I will never stop loving you.'

'It's the same for me. I've loved you for so long now it's a part of me,' he said. 'I can't believe I almost didn't recognise it until it was too late. Now I know it can never be too late for us.'

Her heart skittered. She would never get tired of hearing that.

'It's painful to think about,' Nathan said in between kisses. 'If I hadn't been such a fool when my dad left, and spouted that nonsense about love and marriage, we could have been together all this time.'

'Perhaps,' Saira acknowledged. 'But maybe it's better this way. You were my whole world and I was too young and naive to keep my feelings in proportion. They were all-consuming. But our past and what we've gone through has shaped us. A deep and passionate love doesn't have to burn out any more than a slow, soft love is going to last for ever. I needed to learn so

I could appreciate all the many aspects of the way I feel about you. I've grown in the last few years—definitely in the last couple of months. You've challenged me and supported me to become the woman I am now.'

'"Past is prologue,"' he said with a smile, repeating the phrase she'd used all those months ago.

'Finally, you realise I'm always right,' she said, laughing.

Nathan couldn't stop thinking of how close he'd come to losing all this because of his fears.

'Saira…?' he said.

She murmured, indicating that she'd heard him.

'I was thinking about meeting my dad. Do you think that's a good idea?'

'I think maybe that's exactly what you need.'

'Would you go with me?'

She was silent. Then, 'If you need or want me to, of course I will. But it may be something you need to do on your own the first time.'

'And what if I decide I don't want to stay in contact? That I don't want our daughter to know him?'

'Then I'll know that will be the best decision for our daughter.' She spoke without hesitation, and in a matter-of-fact way, making it clear her love was unconditional.

He was usually the one who supported other people. It humbled him to recognise that Saira would always be there to support him.

He bent his face to kiss her, before drawing her back to rest her head against his shoulder, fully content and secure in their future.

She giggled suddenly.

'What's so funny?' he asked.

'I'm thinking you'll have to leave your club. I'm not sure you'll qualify as a Six-Month Man much longer.'

'I never qualified for that club,' he said pressing a kiss to her temple. 'I've been in love with you for much longer than six months.'

'Oh…' she said, her eyes sparkling with unshed tears.

She drew his face into her hands, leaning up to give him a deep, passionate kiss.

After they broke for air, he interlaced his fingers through hers. 'Much as I hate to spoil the mood, we still need to make a few decisions. Do you want to carry on house-hunting now, or are you happy to stay here until after the baby's born?'

'I like this house. It's an amazing gesture you made, Nate. We can wait until after the baby's born to buy a place, but maybe we should continue to look at houses. Not that I expect we'll find a place that suits us better. But I insist I pay my share of the rent.'

He grinned. His independent woman. He knew better than to argue.

'Agreed.'

He bent forward to cover her mouth, felt their kiss deepening, flaring into passion. It was only when he sensed they were slipping off the couch that he broke apart.

'Enough. We still have things to discuss. You can't distract me with sex.'

'I'm willing to bet otherwise,' she said with a grin, running her fingers down his chest.

'If you don't behave, you're going to have to sit at the other end of the couch,' he replied, drawing her closer again.

'Okay, you win,' she said, snuggling into him. What do you want to talk about?'

'We agreed I would move in in a few weeks before the baby's due. Do you still want to keep to that plan?'

He knew she loved him, but she was still worried about the pregnancy. If she thought his moving in earlier would tempt fate he wouldn't do it.

She tilted her head, as if appraising him. What was going through her mind?

'It's a big house,' she said. 'I imagine it could be scary if I was here on my own all the time.'

He grinned. 'I see. Do you think if I move in with you it would be less scary?'

'Well, you'll still be travelling a lot for busi-

ness before the baby's due, won't you? I don't
want you under my feet all the time.'

They both laughed at the idea that was even
a possibility with the amount of space in the
house.

'I'd like you to move in whenever you can,'
Saira said, 'but I know it's easier for you to be
in London for work, so don't come before you
planned to if it's less convenient.'

'If you're happy for me to be here, I can move
in this weekend.'

He wasn't his father. He wouldn't put his business over his family. He would find a way to
make it work.

She burrowed into his chest, fitting him perfectly, as always. He couldn't remember a time
when he'd been happier. There was only one
thing that could make it more perfect.

'Saira,' he began softly, 'does this mean you'll
marry me?'

He cursed under his breath when she pulled
away from him, straightened up, then put her
legs back on the floor. 'No, it doesn't,' she answered with a slight laugh.

'Why not?' he asked, surprise in his voice.

She reached up to cup his face. 'I don't feel
the need to get married at the moment.'

'But—'

'Nate, I love you. I'm not going to leave you

and I know you're always going to be there for me. With the baby, we're committed to each other in every way possible. We don't need to be married to prove that,' she said, staring deeply into his eyes.

'You said earlier you would marry me.' She wouldn't have lied to him. What had changed her mind?

'And maybe one day I will. Nate, I'm not saying never. I'm saying not now. We don't want to steal Miranda's thunder. There's no rush.'

'One day, though?' he asked, needing reassurance.

'Nate, you're not going to get rid of me—ever. I'm not going anywhere. You have to believe that. You have to trust me. And, more importantly, you have to trust yourself.'

'I do trust you.'

It was as simple as that. He trusted her, and because she believed in him, he believed too. Because she was Saira.

'I'll have to wait until you ask me, then?'

She winked. 'That sounds right to me.'

He could be patient. He'd waited for her before—he could do it again.

'Marriage doesn't give us any guarantees,' she said, staring deeply into his eyes. There was no hiding the sincerity in them. 'Forever, happily-ever-after... Those take a leap of faith.'

'I know,' he replied. 'I've never taken that leap before, though.'

'That's all right,' she said, taking his hands in hers. 'You're not doing it alone. I'll be leaping with you.'

EPILOGUE

A year later

STANDING IN THE kitchenette of the hotel suite at Haynes Mayfair, overlooking the living area, Saira clasped her hands to her heart. Everyone she cared about was in one place. Her parents had broken their stay in India to be here, as well as her brothers, their families and Nathan's family.

His sisters were still in touch with his father, who'd attended Miranda's wedding but hadn't been asked to give the bride away. Over the past year Nathan had met with his father on a few occasions. He hadn't invited his father to today's ceremony, but they were continuing to work on their relationship. Saira supported Nathan's decisions regarding when and how his father might be welcomed into their lives, knowing that Nathan was open to giving his father a chance, and believed his father wanted to and was capable of change.

The Six-Month Men were there too, breaking off from their habitual half-yearly get-together to support Nathan.

All were gathered around Jaan, her and Nate's seven-month-old daughter, watching her having her first solids ceremony. She was gurgling and in her element, lapping up the attention while sitting safe and secure on Nathan's lap. He paid no attention to the tiny food-covered hand gripping his tie, or the globs of rice over his suit.

The past few months had been practically perfect. Apart from being a couple of weeks overdue, Jaan's birth had gone smoothly, and she was generally a content child. Nathan had taken a few weeks off after the birth, adapting to fatherhood as easily as he did anything else he turned his mind to.

Now he travelled less frequently and worked from home regularly. As he often told her, he used to enjoy travelling because he had nothing to stay home for. Now he had something more important waiting for him than work.

In a few weeks she would be working from home too. She'd accepted a position with Bastien's family foundation to encourage a learning initiative to empower girls. She was doing it on a voluntary basis, but it would provide the intellectual challenge she wanted.

Who would have thought that in the space of eighteen months she would have changed from being someone convinced independence and having a career were her only focus in life, and relationships were an unnecessary distraction, to being the person she was now, content to be a mother, working as a volunteer and deeply in love with an amazing man.

Nathan came into the kitchen and wrapped his arm around her waist. He pressed a kiss against her temple before turning to look at Jaan. She drank in every detail of the expression of pure adoration and devotion on his face as he watched his daughter. She took in a deep, shaky breath, burying her head in his chest as emotions engulfed her.

'Hey, what's this?' Nathan asked, running a thumb under her eye to catch the teardrops.

'I'm so happy right now,' she whispered.

'Me too.'

They stood peacefully wrapped in each other for a few moments before turning to their guests.

'Everyone's here,' Nathan said. 'It's time.' He stared deeply into her eyes. 'Are you sure you want to do this?'

'Never been more sure of anything in my life.'

The smile he gave on hearing her reply was so full of love and close to complete joy. She hoped it would never change.

'I love you.'

'I love *you*.'

He bent to kiss her fully on the mouth before

taking her hand as they walked to the centre of the room, taking their daughter from his mother.

'Saira and I are so happy and grateful you're here today, celebrating Jaan's Mukhe Bhaat.'

Saira's family cheered at Nathan's perfect pronunciation of the Bengali name for the ceremony.

He continued. 'I know some of you are wondering why we decided to have Jaan's ceremony at this hotel rather than our house. It's because her first solids isn't the only event we're celebrating today.'

Saira smiled at the various expressions of their family and friends, some of them already guessing what was about to happen.

Nathan clasped her hand in his and brought it to his lips. 'Saira and Jaan fill my world completely. I am already the luckiest, happiest man on the planet. But after many, many, many, *many…*' He grimaced as Saira nudged him playfully with her elbow. 'Many months,' he reiterated, giving her a mock stern look, 'On New Year's Eve Saira finally asked me to marry her. And naturally I said yes. I didn't want to give her time to change her mind, so we're getting married today—downstairs in the Regent Ballroom—in an hour.'

The next sixty minutes passed in a haze of activity as their guests got ready—either freshening up or picking out new outfits from the designer boutiques in the hotel. Miranda, the only person they'd let in on their plans, kept Saira steady and calm—the same way Saira had done for her on her wedding day.

Saira had chosen to wear a lengha in traditional red, with ornate gold embroidery—exactly the kind of dress she'd dreamed of wearing on the day of her wedding to Nathan when she was a nineteen-year-old, first learning what love was.

Her vision blurred as she walked towards where Nathan was waiting for her in front of the registrar. Dreams could come true, and in only a few more breaths hers were about to be fully realised.

She was barely aware of repeating the words which would unite her with Nathan before the registrar pronounced them husband and wife.

'At last,' Nathan whispered, before meeting her lips with his in a kiss sealing their future together.

* * * * *